BIRD HUNTER

As a youth, Bird Hunter, a Comanche brave, had had visions of a white man who would be his 'medicine'. The visions become reality when he meets Lars Swensen. Though the big Swede and the Comanche warrior are on opposite sides of a bloody conflict, their friendship is destined to endure. And when Bird Hunter lays near death, struck down by an Osage warrior's axe, only the Swede can save him . . .

BIRD HUNTER

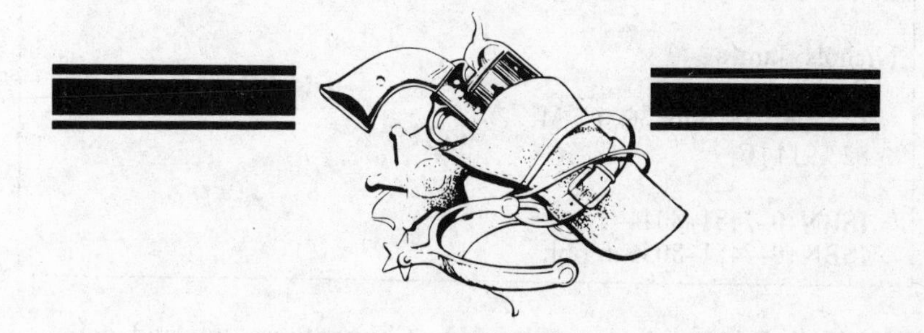

James and C. M. Nichols

ATLANTIC LARGE PRINT
Chivers Press, Bath, England.
Curley Publishing, Inc.,
South Yarmouth, Mass., USA.

Library of Congress Cataloging-in-Publication Data

Nichols, James.
Bird hunter / James and C. M. Nichols.
p. cm.—(Atlantic large print)
ISBN 0–7927–0508–4 (lg. print)
1. Comanche Indians—Fiction. 2. Large type books. I. Title.
[PS3564.I25B5 1991]
813′.54—dc20 90–48276
CIP

British Library Cataloguing in Publication Data

Nichols, James
Bird hunter.
I. Title II. Nichols, C. M.
823.914 [F]

ISBN 0–7451–8044–2
ISBN 0–7451–8056–6 pbk

This Large Print edition is published by Chivers Press, England, and Curley Publishing, Inc., U.S.A. 1991

Published by arrangement with Dorchester Publishing Co., Inc

U.K. Hardback ISBN 0 7451 8044 2
U.K. Softback ISBN 0 7451 8056 6
U.S.A. Softback ISBN 0 7927 0508 4

For Dana, Devlin, Keith, Melanie and Dennis

PREFACE

The valley formed by Buffalo and Cypress Creeks echoed with the war cry of the Comanche. Charging down the hill toward a Texas ranch house silhouetted by a burning barn, the braves rode low over their horses' withers to make themselves a smaller target. To the rancher and his family inside the house, it must have sounded like a large war party. In reality there were but three men—Stealer of Army Horses, a carefree, fearless man; Squirrel, equally without fear but small and as skilled at war as a badger; and their leader, Bird Hunter, a brave war chief honored by Peta Nocona of the Nocona Comanches, Little Mountain, chief of chiefs of the Kiowa, and by his own chief of chiefs, Falcon Man of the Kwahadie Comanches.

When the Osage raiders attacking the ranch house saw the three Comanches, it was too late to take cover. Bird Hunter turned his mount to charge a second time. He saw an Osage warrior whirl. With all his strength, the enemy hurled his axe. It struck Bird Hunter's horse and caromed up into the chief's chest. Heavily, rider and mount fell together and were still.

*   *   *

'Red Feather . . . Black Feather . . . daughter of Dataha.' Over and over he repeated the words. It was late afternoon and the world was silent except for the muttering of the big Indian who lay swathed in fever. His body was still. Only his head rocked back and forth keeping time with the words. 'Red Feather . . . Black Feather . . . daughter of Dataha.'

'I don't think he will live out the night, Lars,' Alfa Swensen said to her husband as they stood over his bed looking at their Kwahadie Comanche friend, Bird Hunter. 'If we only knew what he meant. All day, he has repeated those words.' She wiped his face gently. 'It's partly our fault. He didn't have to come to our rescue.'

Lars searched Bird Hunter's face for some sign of recognition. But Bird Hunter's glazed eyes were focused on a distant time and place.

In his fevered mind he was a boy again searching for his big medicine . . .

CHAPTER ONE

It was the year of the white man's war with Mexico in the Moon of the Falling Leaves. The white man called it November, 1846. To the untrained eye, the young man sitting alone on the crest of the hill seemed a part of the landscape. This was a very important time for a Comanche boy of fourteen. A time for entry into manhood. From this day forward, he would no longer be a boy. His time for toy knives and bows was over. When he returned to the village, he would enter the lodge of the novice. He would no longer live in the lodge of his parents. His father, Slayer of Enemies, was proud, but his mother was afraid for him.

Being a novice was a difficult time of life, a time of conversion. He would ride with the men and learn their ways. No longer would his quiver carry only arrows for birds. He would stalk the bears and the buffalo, raid the horse herds of the Osage, and sit at the council fires even though he would have no voice. This was the way of men. His bow would help protect the women and children of the tribe as he had been protected. That, too, was the way of men.

Lifting his arm he prayed to the Great Spirit to show him the way. After his prayers, he waited. He could leave this place and go in any direction. But only one way would lead him to the spirit that would govern his life and become his medicine. It was there now, waiting for him. He would recognize it, as others before him had found theirs. If he went in the wrong direction he would never find his medicine.

Slowly the man-child rose and stood silently waiting. He was taller than most boys his age by almost a head. His chest was broader. Already he could wear shirts his mother had made for his father. His hair, so black it reflected blue light, hung below his broad shoulders as he watched and listened.

It came to him in a song. A bird song. Swooping low, the tiny creature whistled. It was a yellow finch. All men know a finch does not fly so high. There were no streams nearby; there was no brush for him to nest in; there was nothing to attract the finch to the high barren place. This was his sign.

No one was more alert to the habits of birds. He had killed many of them to fill the cook pot for his mother. Thus he was called Bird Hunter.

He would follow the path of the finch. That path led him south along the lowlands of the deep, coarse grass. Reed-like blades cut his chest and legs as he walked south. He could no longer see the finch, but it had pointed the way. When night came, he lowered himself to the cool ground to sleep, weary from walking.

Sounds of life awakened him and stiffly he rose. The sun was already in full view but its rays still had not found their way through the tall grass to the cool ground below. Taking a sip from his almost-empty water bag, he was thirsty enough to drink it all . . . but that was the way of a child. And his way now was the way of men. Men never emptied their water bags completely because there might be a greater need later. He could see willows ahead and foliage that required water, a promising sign. Also, he could see birds in the sky. Below the flight path of the birds, he would find water.

Finding the river as he expected, he lay down on his stomach and drank his fill. Lying so close to the water, he could hear the sounds that traveled along its surface. He heard horses shifting their weight and white men talking. Slowly he crept along the river until he came to their camp. From his hiding place in the reeds, he watched. Their ways were strange. He could not tell what they were doing as they worked with their teams. Four of the long eared horses, called mules, were backed up to a wagon and hitched with rings of iron forming chains. He could not understand the white-man words. Their language sounded like the clucking of wild prairie chickens.

One man stood out above the rest. He was very tall, his hair yellow like the finch. Unlike the other sour-faced men, he laughed frequently. They called him Swede.

When the wagons were hitched and the other men sat on the high wagon seats, the one called Swede looked directly at Bird Hunter and motioned toward some meat left on a skewer over the dying fire. Swede gave Bird Hunter a friendly wave and climbed to the back of a phenomenally large grey horse. He turned and looked back at Bird Hunter. His eyes were as blue as the sky behind his head. With a half-smile, he rode out to overtake the wagons.

Bird Hunter rose and walked cautiously to their abandoned camp. The smell of cooked meat hung in the air. His stomach growled. He had not eaten since the morning of the night before. Lifting a chunk of meat, he held it to his nose and savored the aroma as it awakened his stomach. He ate ravenously, occasionally thinking of the white man called Swede.

Sitting beside the dying fire, Bird Hunter wondered if the white man could be his medicine. His grandfather had been called White Eagle. His medicine was a powerful white eagle that built its nest within easy reach of the young man seeking his manhood. The stories of the old man's death came to him vividly. A song was still sung around the fires about his grandfather:

Let the Osage beware, for the Eagle waits,
He stands with spear and axe their life to take
Lo, the Eagle waits.
The enemy who has no fear of death,
Come forward now and feel his wrath.

The Comanches returned safely to their village to sing this song around their fires because White Eagle had made his stand. When the Osage came on a hunting party beyond the forks of the two big rivers, they numbered as many as the leaves on a small tree. Swooping down out of the sun, they had killed two women and two men with the swiftness of a diving hawk. Charging into the buffalo herd, they had attacked the hunters, most of whom were on foot. Several Comanche hunters were killed before they could gain their horses and make a stand. It was then that White Eagle shouted for the remaining hunters to follow him into a deep valley. When the young men and women had passed, White Eagle removed his moccasins, took up his lance and axe, and waited.

A cool wind fanned his long grey hair, and his wrinkles multiplied as he smiled with confidence. At first the Osage pulled their mounts uncertainly to a stop in front of the old warrior waiting for them. Each seemed reluctant to make the charge, afraid he would be the one to die, knowing there stood a man ready for death.

'Come!' he challenged. 'Unless you fear the oldest of the Comanche. I wait. I am old and I tire easily standing here without a horse. My bones grow weary and I thirst. I thirst not for water but for the blood of the Sage. If there is a man among you, let him come. For White Eagle is here.' The old man threw back his head, and his scornful laugh echoed through the little valley.

'Come! There is no need to fear dying. Everyone must. Your fathers have, many of them at the hands of White Eagle.'

For a moment he lapsed into silence and those he protected gained the start they needed to make their escape. Then he began again.

'Are Osage warriors women? Is there not one man among you? If so, let him come forward now, and I promise to kill him quickly. He will not have to cry and crawl in the dirt.' He waited in silence for a moment, then added, 'If there is to be no dying, then I must find my moccasins. My village is a long walk for an old man.'

He took a few steps over the sharp rocks toward his buffalo-skin moccasins. Blood marked his foot prints as the first Osage brave charged. With a smile on his face, White Eagle turned to meet him. Four or five of the other Osage braves quickly followed.

When White Eagle was dead, the Osage did

not cut off his head but left his old body intact. When the Comanche people claimed his body, they found a young Osage brave waiting with the old warrior. 'I place my life in Comanche hands to guard the body of a brave man against the vultures. We did not take his head because he is a great warrior. The wives of three of our best men will mourn because of him.' After the young Osage told them the story of White Eagle's death, he was allowed to leave and the story of White Eagle was remembered by the Comanche *and* the Osage.

★ ★ ★

Bird Hunter knew that if he dreamed of the white man when he slept, he would have found his medicine. Saving part of the meat for later, he sprang up and eagerly ran toward the fork in the river. He ran most of the day to return to his village. He ran through the flat lands covered with tiny blue and yellow flowers. A small herd of buffalo parted for the runner. The giant bull pawed the ground at this interruption in his peace, but turned back to his grazing.

As the sun was sinking beyond the horizon, he arrived at his village. No one spoke as he made his way to the lodge of the novice where everything he owned would be waiting for him and there would be presents.

When he entered his lodge, he saw first a long bow made for him by his father. Beside it was a soft skin shirt from the hands of his mother. Sitting beside the new treasures, he tested the strength of the bow and was pleased. This fine weapon was not a boyhood toy. It had great power.

He removed from his waist bag the rest of the meat left by the white man and held it in his hands. In the pouch against his body all day, the warmth still lurked in the food. Slowly raising it to his mouth, he tested it. He would dream of the white man. He would see him again.

With his stomach finally at peace, he stretched out on his buffalo robe and slept. Just before the sun began to climb in the sky, he dreamed of the big white man with the yellow hair and blue eyes and the grey horse. When he opened his eyes, he expected to see the white man standing in his lodge. But it was Kato, his friend, just inside the door of the tipi. Slowly Kato sank to his knees.

'Bird Hunter, I saw nothing. There is no medicine out there for me. I will die in my first battle,' Kato said thickly. 'What of you, Bird Hunter? Did you find what you sought?'

Bird Hunter told him of the white man, the food and the dream.

'A white man cannot be your medicine. You might have to fight that white man. Then how can your medicine help you?'

'I will not fight that white man. Already I know that he will be a friend when again our paths cross. He left the meat for me. I will not fight this man, ever.'

'Even a white man is better than finding no medicine,' Kato said with a sigh.

'My father never found his medicine, and he has lived many years.' Bird Hunter spoke proudly of his father. 'He has been in many battles against the Osage, the Mexicans, the white. But their weapons have never touched him, and he has counted many coups.'

'Your father is a better warrior than most men. There has been no reason for him to have strong medicine.'

'Then you must develop much skill as a fighter. Already you ride as well as most of the men. Although you are smaller than I, you have often beaten me when we wrestle. And you can throw the spear as far as I can.'

'But you shoot arrows farther and truer than I,' Kato said, wanting to exchange compliments.

'Only because my arms are longer and I can draw the bow farther than you. We will grow, both of us. There is a good chance you will catch up with me. My father has told me your father was the largest man at the council fires. You will be like him,' Bird Hunter assured his friend.

His heart lifting, Kato's thoughts turned excitedly in another direction. 'We can claim a wife, Bird Hunter. Who will be your choice?'

'We cannot claim a wife until we have been accepted as men among men.'

'That will be soon.'

'Let's hope it will be soon. We must first prove ourselves. Against the Osage, most likely. Then we can take their horses and buy a wife. To me there are many things more important first.'

'Name some.' Kato leaned forward to hear his friend's answer.

'Making a place for ourselves among the warriors and later among the chiefs is more important. Accumulating a large herd of horses. Helping to feed the widows of our people during the cold moons so their children will sing praises in front of their lodges and all people will know we are good providers. That is more important.'

'Having someone to warm our blankets is also important,' Kato argued. 'We can eat at the fires of the widows but what of the long nights when snows pile high around the lodges? What then? Will you be content to build up your fires and warm your back with that alone?'

'If I must. There is no one I would pick now to marry. Maybe in the spring there will be someone at the north end of the river when we follow the buffalo. Someone I have not yet seen. Someone who will laugh, sing and dance. Someone who can sew and make a robe for me. Perhaps later.'

'You should be called Dreamer. You will have to ask the widows for food and burrow into the ground for warmth like the weasel.'

'Maybe. But I want to be forever happy with the one I pick. I will not have to capture horses and be trading them forever for more wives. I do not care to be called Many Wives, like your uncle.'

'I see nothing wrong with that. There will always be warm, willing partners for your bed if you have many wives.'

'You are the dreamer. You dream of things you know nothing of. When you marry, you will have to go back to the lodge of your uncle to find out what you must do. You may even have to come to me so I can show you what is expected.'

Kato sprang to his feet but changed the subject. 'Come, let's try the new bows. My uncle, Many Wives, made one for me also. We will ride where the wild pigs come to the river to drink. I will kill one before you do even though you can shoot farther than I. We will have the Arrow Maker show us what is best for our bows and we can make many arrows.'

* * *

When there were still patches of snow in the

Moon of the Greening Grass, the tribe of Bird Hunter moved north following the banks of the river. Bird Hunter impatiently rode one of his father's horses, still having no wealth of his own. During the winter he had hunted with the other men and had brought deer to the lodge of his mother, but he wanted to make a lodge of his own. He wanted to move away from the lodge of the novice and make his own among those of the braves. Soon, very soon, he hoped he would get that chance.

They were now approaching the spot along the river where he had seen the white man, Swede. He scanned the distance for sight of him. Someday he was sure he would see him again.

As he watched the horizon, the chief rode up beside him. There was always a tightness in his stomach, an awe, when the chief was nearby.

'You seem to be looking for something,' Falcon Man said.

Bird Hunter told him of his search for the white man.

Falcon Man was wise. Many songs were sung at the fires about his bravery. He was the leader of the Kwahadies and picked his war chief well. Bird Hunter was very proud that his father, Slayer of Enemies, sat on the right hand of Falcon Man.

'This white man, if he is your medicine,

may never come to you again except in dreams. Have you dreamed of him since the first night?'

'As many times as I have fingers.'

'That is a good sign. You may be right that he is your medicine. But it will do you no good if you are looking for him so intensely that an old man like me can ride up on you. You must have patience while you wait for him to find you. You must pay more attention to what is happening around you.'

'Yes, I will. Never again will anyone approach me without my knowing.'

'Then one day you will be a man among men!' Falcon Man rode ahead. The thongs of Bird Hunter's shirt strained with the swelling of his chest.

While the women made camp, the men laid plans for their hunt. The leader of Bird Hunter's party was a tall, thin brave named Deoco. Deoco had great eyesight, could see grazing buffalo long before other men. The young Bird Hunter was glad to be selected for Deoco's party.

'When the first sliver of sun is seen,' said Deoco, 'we will go. With snow still on the ground for them to eat, the buffalo will not need the river. We will hunt them where they are.' He pointed north toward the broad prairie. He slapped one of the older men on the back. 'Go now and make happy your wives, for you will not see them for many suns.'

The other men laughed at his remarks and walked with haste toward their lodges. Bird Hunter rose and walked into the darkness of the night outside the circle of the firelight. He could sense the presence of someone among the trees. Slowly he walked toward a movement in the thicket. He crept slowly forward. From behind a tree he stepped suddenly into the path of the intruder. It was a girl. She did not seem frightened.

'Why are you here in the dark?'

'Why should I tell you? I don't know you.' Curiously she asked, 'Did you come with those from the south? What is your name?'

'My name is Bird Hunter. And yes, I came from the south. Now *you* answer *my* question. What are you doing here?'

'Thinking.'

'You must come into the woods to think? What are your thoughts that you must hide them in the dark?'

'I think of my husband.'

'Why are you not at his fire? You should be there to feed and comfort him before the hunt.'

'There is nothing I would like better. But my husband is dead. I have become a burden to my sister's husband. Even now, as she bids him goodbye as a good wife does, I must walk here in the shadows, not to disturb them.'

'You can bid me goodbye.' His words were

not meant to be suggestive, and he was already embarrassed at the boldness of her remarks, but now that the words were there between them, he pretended a braveness he did not feel.

'You are a boy. Height and breadth alone do not make you a man. You have never held a woman. What do you know about saying goodbye to one?'

'It is the duty of the older people to teach the young,' he said winningly. 'You are older and can teach me how to say goodbye.'

'I am not so old that I should become the teacher of children. I am not much older than you but I am a woman.'

'If you are too young to teach, then you are too young to talk so old.' Taking another step toward her, he stood as rigid as the tree beside him and waited. Her hand reached out and rested on his shoulder. Then slowly it moved over his chest, soft and tantalizing.

'I order you to live, Bird Hunter, so that you will someday be a warrior who will bring pride to any woman. You are man-tall and before this night is over, you will know how to say goodbye.' Her hand moved to his shoulder and pressed him groundward.

CHAPTER TWO

The foster daughter of the Swensen's wept softly in the corner. Since Bird Hunter's injury she had worked beside Alfa for a day and a night. Now in the second day, she tried to close her ears and her mind to her mother's doubts. The man who had made a good life possible for her was dying and there was nothing she could do.

With her hands pressed tightly over her mouth, she struggled to suppress the sobs.

The muffled sounds reached Bird Hunter's keen ears but in his fevered mind it was . . .

. . . as the night birds long ago awakened him, Bird Hunter stirred and reached for the girl he had met in the woods. But she was gone. Throwing his robe aside, he rose and strained to see into the darkness. He tried to hear her movement in the dark woods. There were only the sounds of night birds and small night animals.

Replacing the soft shirt his mother had made for him, he stood and wrapped his robe around him. Slowly he moved toward the sleeping camp. Suddenly he realized he did not know her name or what she looked like in daylight. All he knew was the feel of her.

When he entered the circle of tipis, many of the women were already preparing their cooking fires. Some of the men left their warm lodges and wandered sleepily into the woods to relieve themselves. Bird Hunter walked in front of the lodges and looked at all of the younger women and wondered. Kato hailed him and ran to meet him.

'I have been so anxious for this day to begin. I was awake most of the night.' He scratched his sides and yawned. 'Where were you? Your bed was empty all night.'

'I slept in the woods.'

'Ah, you are also excited about the hunt! I have learned that Deoco killed three buffalo on *his* first hunt when he was our age. What do you think of that? He killed more than any of the other men on his first hunt. It is no wonder that he is called the best hunter of all men. We are lucky to be with him!'

'Yes, we are. But right now, I am hungry. Have you eaten?'

'No. I will join you at the fire.'

Together they went to the community fire and took food prepared by the older women for novices and men without wives. Sitting crosslegged, they ate wild pig that had roasted in the coals overnight. They watched the eastern sky. When the edge of the sun began to show, they rose and went to their horses, the first ones ready.

Deoco laughed when he saw their eagerness. 'This is as it should be. All men should be standing by their horses instead of trying to appease their women. We will have many more mouths to feed by the time we hunt again because of the long goodbyes.' He laughed again. Taking the horn of the buffalo from his waist, he blew loudly into it. Its bleating sound echoed in the trees. 'We go. They will follow at a full gallop in a few minutes.'

They had gone only a short distance when Bird Hunter looked back and saw the other hunters riding hard behind them to catch up. They laughed and slapped at each other and bragged of their sexual powers. Soon they settled down into a long, silent, single column, alert for the first sign of buffalo.

For three days they traveled in a zigzag course northward. Shortly before sundown on the third day, they were hailed by a band of Kiowa from the ridge of a long range of hills. Deoco rode forward to meet them. The older men had friends among them and renewed old acquaintances. Deoco brought a young Kiowa to Bird Hunter and Kato.

'This is the son of my friend, Two Horses. He too is a novice. Show him the friendship of the Comanche and the three of you can prepare yourselves for the kill. A herd has been sighted beyond the hills. Tomorrow we go among them.' With a gentle hand he urged the young Kiowa forward. 'This is Kato and Bird Hunter. Our Kiowa friend here is called Young Wolf.'

The three new friends squatted beside their fire trying to talk. At first their sun language was halting and stiff, and they laughed at one another's efforts. But by the time they took to their robes for the night, they were beginning to understand one another.

All three were anxious for the night to end so they could get to the hunt.

* * *

Deoco nudged them awake with his toe. 'It is time. Tend to your horse, then yourselves. We go with the ghost light at dawn.'

Rolling from their robes, they ran to their horses, rubbed them down, fed and watered them. When they returned to the fires, they were too excited to eat.

Wisely Deoco badgered them. 'You may not get a chance to eat again until long after the sun has gone to bed.' He pointed at their water bags. 'Be sure they are filled. You may have to share it with your horse.'

Young Wolf waved goodbye to them and joined his own people. His father, Two Horses, waited at the edge of the camp. He clapped his hand proudly on his son's shoulder. The Kiowas were the first to ride out. They circled wide, heading toward the river.

Bird Hunter stood beside his horse waiting for Deoco's order to mount. Swinging easily onto the horse's back, he gave the animal his head and followed the other braves.

Suddenly from the crest of a foothill came a signal that the buffalo had been sighted. Excitement and tension swept through the men at the long-awaited signal. Bird Hunter could feel the muscles tighten in his arms. Along his back crawled ant's feet of anticipation. Deoco motioned for them to halt as he rode ahead to inspect the herd. The seasoned hunters dismounted and ate jerky, sipping from their water bags with a calmness Kato and Bird Hunter could not summon.

'Do you feel fear, Bird Hunter?'

'I'm not sure what I feel. Anxious, yes.'

'And I.' Kato lapsed into silence.

Bird Hunter again inspected the new bow and each arrow. He fingered the sheath at his waist to assure himself he still had the skinning knife. During the long winter months, he had shot the heavy arrows and remembered that he must aim carefully slightly above the target to allow for drop. He remembered also his father's instructions. The buffalo cannot be shot from a distance like deer, but only at close range. 'You must not shoot until you can feel and hear their breath!' his father had cautioned. He wished Slayer of Enemies was with him on this hunt instead of guarding the camp.

Kato nudged him. Deoco returned from the hills and slipped easily off his horse.

'Wakato, take Kato and two others and circle wide. Approach from the dead tree, there. Come in low through the grass. Buffalo graze where the marsh grasses grow. Many Wives will take the men I do not take and go over the hill. There will be no cover for you. Hide yourself with your robes and move as slowly as the shadows. Hold your kill until you see that Wakato and I are among them.'

He studied each face carefully and picked four hunters to go with him. He looked at Bird Hunter for what seemed an eternity before pointing to him also. They turned their horses over to an old man of many names, among them Keeper of Horses and Arrow Maker.

Deoco's band walked upright until they reached the crest of the hill. They slid along the ground on their bellies like snakes when they neared the top. Deoco signaled for them to spread out. Skillfully he pulled his robe over his head and drew into it. Bird Hunter watched Deoco and mimicked every move. In a hunched position, they eased over the hill. Bird Hunter was startled to see how close they were to the herd. He could hear the breathing of the big animals, as his father had said. He could feel the heat from their bodies!

A big cow lifted her head and studied him until a calf nuzzled her udder. She lowered her head with indifference and continued to graze. Bird Hunter moved stealthily up beside a young bull.

He waited and watched Deoco eagerly.

Deoco nodded to Bird Hunter and released an arrow from his bow. The arrow sank deeply into the chest of a large bull, behind his left foreleg. Bird Hunter aimed his own arrow to hit a young bull in the chest behind the left foreleg. Half its length disappeared into the matted fur. The bull's head snapped hard to the left. Bird Hunter fitted another arrow to the string. Slowly the bull made a quarter turn, facing him. Bird Hunter moved again to the side. The bull continued to turn with him. After a third attempt to outflank the wounded animal, he drew his bow to the full length of the arrow and let it fly. The string whipped against his arm. He could feel blood inside his new shirt, but he kept his eye on the buffalo. At first he thought he had missed. Then he saw the feathers protruding from the neck. Blood dripped from the black nostrils. When the stunned beast opened his mouth to breathe, blood flowed freely.

Bird Hunter waited. There was nothing more he could do. In spite of its wounds, the huge animal turned painfully with him each time he tried to get a shot into the heart. Fingering the knife at his side, he wondered frantically if he should get in close enough to cut the throat. Suddenly the bull snorted, spraying blood all over Bird Hunter. Slowly his knees buckled, he sank forward, and rolled over on his side. Bird Hunter glanced up with uncertainty, and Deoco gave him an approving sign. He made a sign across his throat with his thumb. Bird Hunter stepped in close and slit the bull's throat.

His first kill. He felt great excitement and relief. He spied a cow and moved toward her. Deoco shook his head, a message for him to let it lie. Bird Hunter headed for another young bull. With the first shot, the animal twisted hard to the left and dropped dead almost at his feet. The earth trembled when the shaggy body fell.

Suddenly there was a great clap of thunder which startled Bird Hunter. Thunder would frighten the herd. Uneasily he glanced around him at the animals. Almost as one body they began to move. A cow and her calf almost trampled Bird Hunter. Another loud clap of thunder tore the air, and Bird Hunter heard a roaring behind him. There was a tremor in the ground. The lead bull had given the alert, and they were running. Bird Hunter leaped for cover behind the first bull he had killed. He hunched to the ground quickly. The ground shook like an earthquake with hundreds of hoof beats.

All around him churned buffalo stampeding to the river. It seemed like hours that he pressed against the side of the smelly animal. In death the bull had saved the life of its own assailant. When at last the sound of running hooves died away, Bird Hunter cautiously raised his head.

Other members of the hunting party had also sought cover behind black carcasses. Many Wives stood trembling over the body of a young bull. Deoco called, 'What is it, Many Wives?'

'It is Towanda. He is dead.'

With masked expressions, each hunter filed by to look at Towanda's body. Bird Hunter felt Deoco's hand on his shoulder. 'Come, we must pay respects to a brave man.'

Together they went to the dead man's side. Bird Hunter's stomach muscles tightened. He had never seen death like this. Always before it was clean. An old man dying in his sleep or a child in his mother's robes. Never like this. Towanda's arms were twisted and broken. His head was crushed and bloody where many hooves had struck him. Towanda's brother dropped sorrowfully to his knees. Bird Hunter strode quickly away, his hand over his mouth. Kato also stood apart from the others, his face distorted.

'Friend Kato, the hunt is destroyed for me.'

'Yes. There is no way to express how I feel. It has been in my heart to ask for the hand of Towanda's sister Dataha when I can afford a wife. My heart now goes out to her. She will grieve as no other, for he was her favorite brother.'

'I did not know of your feelings for Towanda's sister. She is still a girl.' Bird Hunter studied his friend. 'Now is the time for you to help her. In her time of loss she will be in need of friends.'

'I don't want to be her friend. I want to be her husband. With the coming of the Moon of Deep Grass, she will be a woman. It was then that I had hoped to talk to Towanda.'

'Then you should talk to her brother, Nacato, when he has finished his time of grieving.' They turned and looked at the man who knelt beside his dead brother, beating his chest. He was the man most feared among their tribe.

'Nacato places more importance on wealth than Towanda. I must be rich to face him.'

'Then we will make you rich.'

Kato looked at his friend with wonder. He did not understand the meaning behind Bird Hunter's dark eyes.

'We will seek the Osage and take from them the horses we need to make you rich. Then you can help Dataha. She will be pleased to have a rich man ask for her hand.'

'Will you help me so much?'

'We have been friends for longer than we can remember. There is but one purpose for friends. Your feelings for Dataha surprise me. I felt we kept nothing from each other. Is there more that you have kept in your heart and mind? Why have you said nothing?'

'I feared you would laugh at me.'

Placing his arm around the shoulder of his friend, Bird Hunter looked at him as he would a brother. 'I would laugh at your attempts to whistle or sing. There are many things that you might say I would laugh at. But I would never laugh at what is in my friend's heart.'

For a moment Kato was deep in thought. 'This, then, is my heart speaking. If I should die during our raid, will you ask for the hand of Dataha? I would rest more easily with the spirits if I knew she was to marry you. She will need someone who is strong and kind.'

'I have no wish for a wife. There is much to learn about women. As much as there is to learn about horses or making war.' He paused, then added. 'Maybe more.'

They watched solemnly as the body of Towanda was wrapped in his robe. Keeper of Horses brought forward Towanda's horse. The men lifted the body to the back of the horse and Nacato led it away. He would return to the village. There would be much crying among the women. They would tear their hair and beat the ground. They would pray to the sky and spit in the fires.

* * *

The piles of meat and robes grew larger when the women arrived to skin and dress the kill.

When they had prepared enough meat and skins for the long months ahead, all was loaded onto travois and slowly hauled to the village.

Deoco rewarded Bird Hunter for his successful hunting. 'Your name shall become Killer of Buffalos. What do you think of that?' Deoco asked. 'Bird Hunter is more the name of a boy than a man.'

'I will not question the wishes of my elders. But I like the name I bear. My mother likes it as well,' Bird Hunter said with reservation.

'If it is not your wish, then your name will not be changed. You can for all your life be known as Bird Hunter, if that is your desire. Whatever you are called, you will be known and respected by all of our people, the Nocona, the Yamparika, the Penatekas, and the Kwahadies.'

Bird Hunter sat his horse with the words of Deoco still ringing in his ears. To be called Killer of Buffalos by a man like Deoco surely meant he was no longer a novice. He was at last treated as a man, by a man among men.

CHAPTER THREE

'Red Feather . . . Black Feather . . . Yellow Finch . . . daughter of Dataha.' Bird Hunter's head rolled and he licked his feverish lips.

'Horses ... for Kato.'

With a sigh he lapsed into silence and for a second there was no breathing. Lars, Alfa and Shanda waited anxiously at his bedside. His breath came and he was silent, dreaming...

There was always keening.

'Tears feed the waters of the world on which men live,' his mother had said when he was still a young man.

Deoco chose Bird Hunter and two other braves to ride with him to the Kiowa camp to say farewell after the hunt. As they approached the crest of the hill above the river, they could hear keening from the camp of their friends. Ahead by fifty yards rode Deoco, the first to meet the tall Kiowa approaching them. Deoco lowered his head as they talked in hushed voices.

Deoco explained to Bird Hunter. 'Tall Man says when the stampede reached this point, the number of buffalos had increased until they equalled the leaves on the trees. Five good hunters were killed, among them my friend Two Horses and his son Wolf.'

Bird Hunter felt the pain of grief at the sound of his new friend's name. He remembered Towanda's torn body and imagined Wolf dying similarly. It was more than his stomach could bear. Galloping off a few paces, he slipped from his horse and was sick. When he regained his composure, he rose and looked into the face of Deoco.

'There is no need to feel shame at being sick over the death of your friend. There is nothing unmanly about grief. I would be pleased to know there are men who will feel sad when I die,' he said, patting Bird Hunter on the shoulder.

Then he raised his arms and looked at the sky. In a voice broken with passion, he said, 'Why? There was thunder, there were clouds. Why was there no rain? Brave men have died and the sky is again clear. Why?'

Deoco turned to Tall Man. They decided to make a burial ground where the stampede had occurred. Others who came upon this land later would know that brave men had died here on the banks of the river and their spirits watch over this place.

The Comanches stayed for the dedication of the burial ground and took part in the dancing. Tall Man sang a chant to the spirit god for the spirit of Towanda as well as for the Kiowa dead. For three days and nights they danced and sang. On the morning of the fourth day, they rode away without looking back.

When they returned to their own village, the time for keening was over. Towanda's grave was beside those of his mother and father and two of his brothers. Comanches were taught by their elders that the next boy baby born would have the spirit of Towanda. In that way he would live forever among them, though his name would never be spoken again.

* * *

Bird Hunter sat listlessly on the banks of the river and watched the fish jump. Even though he had a fish arrow fitted to the string of his bow, he sat motionless not bothering to aim.

His father walked up behind him. 'At the camp fire it was told that you are a good hunter of buffalo, my son. It is also said that you do not want to change your name. Share with me the reason for this.'

'When Deoco first suggested the change, I was pleased. I knew you would be proud.' He thought for a moment, and his father honored his silence. 'There is much I hope to do. Perhaps some day I will do something more worthy of a new name.'

'You seem to have something on your mind. Since your return from the hunt, you have been quiet like a man with deep thoughts.'

'Yes, there is a girl that Kato seeks for the dance of the maidens. He needs horses so he can ask her brother's permission. I wish to help him gather his wealth.' Bird Hunter saw his father's shoulders tighten. He knew it meant a raid for Osage horses.

'There is much danger. Are you ready for it? There are many brave men among the

Osage. They are not all women because we, the Comanche, say they are.'

'I feel ready to face that. My concern has been your reaction. Also I dread the thought of telling Mother. She still sees me as a little boy.'

'Have no fear of that. She will still look at you with the eyes of a mother when she has more grandchildren than she can count. I can manage her. I will remind her that when I was Kato's age, I felt as he does. It was with hope and pride that she watched me ride out then to seek horses so I could ask for *her* hand. I will remind her of those times. It is good that you want to help your friend. But ... what of yourself? There are many beautiful maidens among our people who look your way.'

Bird Hunter lowered his head to avoid his father's eyes. 'There is that feeling in me that calls for a woman, but I am not ready. It is not right to push myself into it.'

'You will know when the time has come. You are a man now. A man must sleep in his own bed. He must cast his own shadow.'

Silently Slayer of Enemies left Bird Hunter to his thoughts. He could not remember his father talking so to him before. Their talk was that of two men, not father and son. He returned the fish arrow to his quiver.

'You can live for a while, fish. When I return you will be larger and more worthy of my efforts.' He rose and looked for Kato.

* * *

Morning cooking fires had burned low when the two rode away from camp. Kato's uncle, Many Wives, stood at the edge of the camp and waved, a smile on his face. Bird Hunter's mother was watching him even though she did not lift her head. Bird Hunter looked for his father but did not see him. He could not understand why he had not come to watch him leave on such a dangerous mission. Then he remembered his father's words. 'I will ask that the spirit guide and protect you.' And he knew where his father was.

Bird Hunter looked toward the hill where the sun came into the sky. His father was there with uplifted arms.

CHAPTER FOUR

The sun beat down directly overhead as the two young men rode north on their second day. They had not spoken since their morning meal. Bird Hunter rode slightly ahead of Kato, watching the distant hills. A muffled sound drifted to him. With a quick but gentle tug on the reins he stopped his horse. Kato opened his mouth to speak and

Bird Hunter placed a silencing finger on his lips.

They listened intently. The sound came again. Cattle. The sound of cattle moving northward beyond the swell to the east. Bird Hunter and Kato turned their ponies and pushed cautiously forward. Slipping easily to the ground, they topped the low hill. Bird Hunter was shocked. He saw a white man with hair the color of the finch in the valley. The man dismounted and removed his hat, running his fingers through his hair, glancing in their direction. It was just as he had done when Bird Hunter hid along the river and watched the white camp on the morning he first saw this white man.

'He is the same!'

'Who?' Kato asked.

'The man I saw when I sought my medicine. The same man, and he has seen us!'

'He does not have eyes that can see over a hill. Not even Deoco has such eyes.'

'He has seen us. I know he has. He has seen us as he saw me the first time.' Bird Hunter rose and stood tall as he looked down at the big man called Swede. Lifting his hand slightly, the man mounted his horse and made a move to meet them.

'He comes,' Kato whispered and fitted an arrow to his bow.

'No, unstring your bow, Kato! This man

will do us no harm.'

'But . . .'

'If I am wrong and he kills you, I will cry. And now I will answer the question you asked some time ago. If you are killed, I will marry Dataha for you.'

'Never let it be said that you did not offer your friendship to the fullest. When Dataha is big with child, I want to have been the one.'

Bird Hunter ignored his friend as he watched Swede. He mounted his horse and rode over the crest of the hill to meet the white man and his cattle.

'Wait,' Kato said. 'It is only right that I be with you when you die.'

'I will not die. This man is good. When I talk to him, I will know he is my friend and my medicine. You stay. I will return.'

'No!' Kato rushed to his horse and was soon beside him.

The white man waited below for them. When they were close enough, Bird Hunter called to him. 'This is the second time I have seen you.'

There was a puzzled expression on Swede's face.

'You left meat on your fire for me beside the river.'

Bird Hunter was surprised when the man spoke in the tongue of the Comanche. 'You have grown since that time. What I saw beside the river was a boy. You are a man.'

'Did you see us this day?'

'Yes.'

'Were you not frightened?'

'No. There is no reason for me to fear another man. Come ride with us. Join us at our fire tonight.' The Swede offered a hand shake. 'If you are traveling north I would be pleased to have you as my guest. My name is Lars Swensen. Some people call me Swede.'

'I heard your friends call you Swede near the river. We ride north toward the cold winds. My name is Bird Hunter. This is my friend, Kato.' Bird Hunter reined his horse to a standstill as another rider approached from the front of the herd. 'Does he understand we are friends?'

'He knows by now.' Swede raised his hand in a salute. 'This is my friend Lawrence McLin. Mac, these are my friends, Bird Hunter and Kato.' Swede spoke in the white man's language but Bird Hunter understood the word 'friends.'

'Mac is helping me drive my herd to the ranch,' Swede said to Bird Hunter.

'Where is that?'

'Where the two creeks flow together into the river.'

'I have been there many times. There is no ranch there.'

'There is no house now but soon there will be a house where the two creeks come together. I will build it.'

'You will build it? That is the job of a woman. That is our way.'

'Whites and Indians have many ways that are different. Have you ever seen the house of a white man?'

'From the hills overlooking the village. Many times my people have watched and wondered what goes on in such a place.' His voice was full of wonder and curiosity. 'It is built so that it *cannot be moved*!'

'You are right, Bird Hunter. Our houses are built with timbers to remain in one place for years. That is the way I will build my ranch. I will raise cattle and many other kinds of animals. I will raise grain and vegetables, all kinds of food for my family.'

'Where is your family?'

'I have none, yet. But I have plans. When I am ready, I will write to my lady and she will come here and we will marry. Then I will have a family.'

'That is why we are here. Kato wishes to marry. We go to get horses so he will have enough wealth to marry. He has much love for Dataha. Even when he sleeps, he calls her name.'

'I do not,' Kato said sheepishly.

'You must stay awake some night and listen. He is like a sick puppy that whimpers and cries in his sleep. This love he feels for her will kill him and I will have to marry Dataha and give her children. We will name all of them Kato, boys and girls alike.' Swede and Bird Hunter laughed. McLin did not understand what was said, and Kato did not think the joke was funny.

'Where did you learn to speak our language?' Bird Hunter asked.

'When I first came to Texas there was a man who had been a trader among your people. His mother was Comanche. He taught me your tongue.'

Mac spoke to the Swede who then turned in the saddle to face Bird Hunter. 'We will make an early camp. Mac feels it will rain soon.'

'He is right,' Bird Hunter agreed. 'There will be rain before it is dark.'

'There is a lot to learn about this country. Where I came from we could sometimes see the rains coming for two days across . . .' Swede groped for a word. There was no word in Comanche for sea. At last he said, 'wide, wide, water.'

'Where do you come from that you can see the rain so long before you feel it?' Bird Hunter questioned. 'Is the water wider than the rivers where they flow together?'

'The land is called Sweden. The water is called Baltic.'

Bird Hunter smiled. 'You must have been a big chief in your land for them to name it after you.' Before Swede could comment, he went on. 'Tell us more of the Baltic waters.

How wide? My horse is a good swimmer, how long for him to swim the waters?'

'I am called Swede because I come from Sweden. They did not name the land for me. The Baltic is so wide man cannot see the other side. It takes four or more days to cross the water. Your horse could not swim so far.'

All of them were enjoying their time together. Swede was anxious to make camp so he could visit more with them. Mac had ridden forward and was heading up the herd. Soon they were standing in a tight group, resting. Mac built a small fire and put coffee on to boil. Swede seemed to want to help the Comanches understand things they had never seen.

'When my books come, I will show you pictures of the Baltic and of my home land.'

Leaning against a rock, he took out his pipe and tamped tobacco into it. 'You are welcome to come to my house and see the books when they arrive. There is much we can learn from each other.'

'Among my people, we teach each other. I will tell my brothers of the white man called Swede and his friend called Mac when I return. I will also tell them of my friend's ranch soon to be built at the fork of the two creeks. In this way, word will pass from one to another. Soon all Comanches, from the lands of the Mexicans to the lands of the Cut Throat Sioux, will know and they will not harm my friend.'

The Swede was pleased with his words.

'I wish it could be the same with my people. But sadly it is not. There are many people who would harm you no matter whose friend you are.'

'There is one thing I do not understand. Why the white men wish to live in one place and raise cattle,' Kato said.

'There are far too many whites for us to live as you do. We must settle in one place and raise food for others who live in large cities ... or villages ... and cannot raise food for themselves.'

Kato studied him for a minute. 'I wondered if you would eat all of the cattle yourself.' Making a sign of a large stomach, he added, 'You would be like one among our people who is called Round Man.'

The Swede translated for Mac and everyone laughed.

Mac opened a bag of hard biscuits and jerky. He passed it to Bird Hunter who took some and studied the cattle grazing nearby.

'Why do you eat dried meat when there is fresh meat there?'

The Swede understood that Bird Hunter was challenging the white man's ways.

'It is wasteful to kill for food when all of it will not be eaten. There are many who do that with the buffalo because the supply seems endless, but the Indian knows better. The men who do this are wrong.'

'Yes,' Bird Hunter agreed. 'The Comanches must go farther all the time to find buffalo for his needs.'

'Bird Hunter could be called Killer of Buffalo if he would change his name,' Kato said.

Bird Hunter dismissed his skills as a hunter. 'We must hunt well or our cooking pots will be empty and my people will starve. We have no one to raise cattle for us and must see to our own needs.'

Mac listened to the conversation, understanding only scattered words. Removing his hat he ran his fingers through his curly red hair.

Kato spoke jokingly to Swede.

'Mac, Kato says you better keep your hat on.' The Swede laughed. 'Your scalp would be a great prize.'

Mac's laugh was not so hearty and he put his hat back on swiftly. The Swede poured coffee and offered it to Kato and Bird Hunter, who sipped the black brew, frowning. When Mac added molasses to their cups, the mixture was more pleasing to their taste.

Bird Hunter smiled. 'What is this called?'

'Coffee.'

'I will remember.' Finishing his coffee, Bird Hunter returned the cup to Mac and rose.

'The shadows are long. We must go if we are to get the horses for Kato.'

'Where do you go for them?'

'The village of Osage. We will take them while they sleep.'

'They will have guards. There will be danger.' There was much concern in the Swede's face when he spoke.

'The taking and the keeping is what gives value to the horse. If they were like dogs that follow anyone who offers them a bone, they would be of no more value than a dog. If we must, we will kill the guards. Then we will take the horses we want. When we return, Kato will be a very rich man. He can marry Dataha and all the maidens he wants. When her brother sees the horses, he will be glad to have his sister marry such a rich man.' Bird Hunter patted his friend's shoulder. 'He is sick with love. If the Osage do not kill him, his yearning surely will.'

Swede and Mac watched them ride away. 'It's a shame all white men and red men don't get along better,' McLin observed.

Tiny dots of rain began to wet the dust around their feet.

* * *

Under a ledge out of the rain, the two friends built a fire and cooked a rabbit for dinner, discussing what Swede had told them. 'It is strange about the number of whites. If there are so many they can not each raise their own cattle or kill game to eat . . .' He paused and studied the fire. 'Where do they all live?'

Kato agreed it was a mystery.

'But Swede has said it is so,' Bird Hunter reminded him. 'We must accept the word of a friend. It is our way.'

Kato shook his head. 'It is too much for me to think about. My concern now is horses.'

The rain stopped.

When they had eaten and Kato slept, Bird Hunter lay and watched stars thoughtfully, as more gradually appeared. Kato was anxious to marry Dataha. The Swede was anxious to build his house and have a wife to share it with him. Bird Hunter remembered how good it felt sleeping beside the young widow before the hunt. There would always be warm, exciting thoughts of her in his mind. He could almost feel her next to him before he slept.

CHAPTER FIVE

'She stands in the water . . . in the water . . . she stands.' His voice faded. There was no sound as his cracked lips continued to move, forming inaudible words.

Shanda replaced the wet towel on his broad

forehead and studied his kind face, which was now twisted with fever and pain. Bird Hunter's hand darted out and caught her forearm. His grip was so tight she could feel the arm going numb but she made no attempt to release herself from him.

'Is he hurting you?' her mother questioned.

'If it helps him, it does not hurt,' Shanda replied.

He murmured, 'She stands . . . Osage . . . in the water.'

* * *

Long before sunup on the fourth morning, Kato and Bird Hunter arrived at the village of the Osage. In the shelter of a low cottonwood tree, they studied the camp. The horse herd grazed in tall grass on a jetty of land extending into the river. The village blocked the only way in or out. They must go through the village to get to the horses. Their dream of riches seemed unattainable.

'I will be an old man and will still be riding a borrowed horse,' Kato muttered. 'The Osage are not childish fools. It would take all the warriors of our village to steal their horses.'

'Maybe not. They may not have a guard. They did not know we were coming and may think they do not need one. They are very unlucky, these Osage, because you and I are here to take all their horses.'

'All?'

'Yes, all! We will wait until tonight. There will be no moon. When it is darkest, we cross the river and circle to the lodges closest to the herd. We will steal the two hardiest mounts for ourselves, then stampede the rest into the river. Horses are not fish. They swim in the easiest direction. What we do not take will run free on the side of the river away from the village. If the Osage follow, first they will have to cross the river to catch the frightened horses. We will be well on our way by that time.'

'But,' Kato protested, 'we will be driving their horses ahead of us. They could still catch us even though we have a day's head start.'

'We can drive riderless horses faster than they can follow.'

'If your name is changed, I think it should be One Who Dreams a Lot, instead of Killer of Buffalo.'

'Even if we only get the two horses to escape on they will know we were here and remember. They will remember the mighty Comanche whose youngest braves are better men then they!'

Kato pointed to a place near the first bend in the river. 'We can wait there where the rushes grow tall enough to hide us. But we must keep our horses quiet.'

Bird Hunter nodded. 'We go now before the sun comes up.'

'If your plan works, we will be the richest among our people. Even Stealer of Army Horses does not have as many horses as I see beyond the river.'

'When we are old and sitting beside the fire chewing meat without teeth, we will tell the children about this day.'

* * *

During the long hours of the day, they hid in the rushes. Kato slept as Bird Hunter lay on his stomach watching a girl who came to the edge of the river to wash her clothes. She washed all of the garments and spread them on bushes to dry. Then she took off the clothes she wore and washed them also. Her nude body was a magnet to his eyes. He could not turn his face away. What he did now was wrong among his people. A man or boy who was caught watching a Comanche girl as he was doing would be whipped by her father or her brother and the guilty peeper would not be allowed to defend himself. This girl was Osage. That seemed to make a bad thing all right. It reminded him of the night he slept beside the young widow without knowing her name or her face. Although this was an Osage girl and an enemy, he could not hate her. She was about his own age. Beautiful, like some of the girls among his own people.

Suddenly, he wished she were dressed and sitting beside him so they could talk. They could tell each other what made them laugh and cry. He could tell her of his mother and she of hers.

She walked into the water to bathe. When she was finished, she left the water and wiped her body with her hands to remove the water. It stirred the fires in him.

Suddenly she turned toward him. He had made no sound. He was sure of that. Or maybe he did without realizing it. There was a sound in his throat that wanted to come out.

Finally turning with her back to him, she dressed slowly and returned without alarm to the village.

* * *

All day his thoughts turned to the girl and it helped the long hours pass. He and Kato had not spoken since dawn. Sound traveled quickly and great distances over water. They were very near the river. Kato must be thinking about Dataha while he was thinking of the Osage girl.

His mind needed to be clear so they would not fail. There would be much singing and dancing if he and Kato returned to their village with so many horses.

Darkness closed in the rushes long before

the sun was gone from the sky. When the first stars appeared, they rose and removed the bridles from their horses and hung them around their waist to put on the Osage horses. Their own mounts would run with the stolen herd and help lead them in the right direction.

Each held onto his horse's mane as they crept from the rushes and stood cautiously on the bank opposite the camp. The fires died one by one and the cold, white smoke blanketed the village long after the last fire died. Still they waited.

'How long?' Kato whispered.

He whispered back. 'Until we are sure the last old men have returned to their lodge after emptying their bladders so they do not warn those who can fight.'

* * *

The night deepened.

Bird Hunter whispered, 'Now!' as he released his horse. They eased together into the water. As expected, Bird Hunter's big grey and Kato's appaloosa stopped when they reached the edge of the water.

Silently dog-paddling, the two friends moved through the water. As they neared the opposite bank, Kato reached out and touched Bird Hunter's shoulder. Less than ten yards away stood a man urinating into the river.

Water splashed against water with the sound of a waterfall. They waited. When he had finished, the old Osage yawned broadly and vanished into the darkness.

Coming out of the water, they stood for a moment and allowed the herd to grow accustomed to their smell. Bird Hunter motioned Kato to go left while he would circle to the right until they met again beyond the herd. Removing his knife from his waist, he circled the herd.

Bird Hunter arrived first since Kato had a longer distance to cover. While he waited, he picked out two of the best-looking steeds with large, thick chests. They would be able to run at top speed without getting winded.

Reins held tightly, Bird Hunter paused, hearing bold movement. Too bold. There was no attempt to be quiet. Standing close to the horse, Bird Hunter waited. He heard a man talking either to another man or perhaps to a horse.

It was a strange language.

Bird Hunter held his breath. Kato might think it was Bird Hunter waiting. Too late he heard Kato whisper to the man. There was no time to think. Bird Hunter lunged forward and sank his knife, as he had been taught, into the man's throat, so that he would not cry out a warning.

The body slid silently to the ground. Kato stood stunned and uncomprehending. Swiftly

Bird Hunter shoved Kato toward one of the roans he had selected for them. Kato recovered and slipped the bridle on the Osage horse. Before Bird Hunter realized his intentions, Kato slit the scalp and lifted the hair lock from the dead man.

They mounted, together let out the war cry of their people, and whipped the herd of horses into stampeding toward the river. They heard the whinny of their Comanche horses on the opposite bank and the captive herd followed. Behind there came another sound. The Osage braves rushed from their lodges to find their horses missing. There was no way for them to know they were losing their herd to only two young braves who had never stolen anything before. They were hesitant to engage in battle with a presumably large war party of seasoned Comanche braves. Bird Hunter laughed, whooped, and made as much noise as he could to keep the horses moving.

They were in the water with a solid mass of horse flesh strung out from bank to bank. Just stealing the roans beneath them was coup enough to be told around the camp fires.

It was almost sunup when they slowed to a walk. During the night they had lost two. But there were still more remaining horses than the fingers and toes of five warriors. They would be the richest braves among all the Kwahadies if they returned with all of them.

He traded the roan for his own big grey. He patted the familiar neck. Kato still rode the roan. He leaned forward suddenly as if in pain. Bird Hunter circled the herd to meet his friend.

'What is wrong, Kato?'

'My foot. There is much pain.' He lifted his right foot to show Bird Hunter.

'What happened? There is so much blood.'

'At the river, one of the Osage warriors overtook me. When I kicked him in the face, he cut my foot with his axe.'

Bird Hunter reined in the grey. 'Put your foot up here on my leg, so I can see it.'

Bird Hunter slowly removed the moccasin. All of Kato's toes but his big one were gone. In a shocked voice he said, 'The toes are here inside your moccasin, Kato.'

Kato looked at the blood-smeared foot. The swelling and tight moccasin had stopped the bleeding. A weak smile crept over his almost colorless face. 'I am grateful he only landed one good blow.'

'How do you feel?'

'A little weak. There is less pain with my foot lifted up. I will ride with it in front of me.' Kato looked at his toes in the moccasin. 'Like so many grubs, they curl up in hiding,' he laughed weakly.

'It is not funny. Should we stop to tend your wound?'

'No. They might overtake us. Surely they

have recaptured some of their horses and are riding hard to catch us even as we linger.'

Kato retrieved his toes from his moccasin. 'When we are back with our people, I will string these and wear them around my neck. I will be the only man alive with toes on his chest,' again he laughed, trying to sound brave.

'If you can ride, I will return to the herd. They are beginning to spread.'

Bird Hunter watched the big grey belonging to his father and the appaloosa belonging to Kato's uncle. They pranced as they led the Osage herd southward toward the Kwahadie camp. It would be a ceremonial day when they sighted their own camp fires. The two lead animals seemed to sense their importance too, strutting ahead of the herd like true Comanches.

* * *

It was noon. They had driven the herd as hard as they could for three days. Smoke lay low over their campsite ahead. Riders came to meet them, Bird Hunter's father in the lead.

Bunching the herd together tightly, Bird Hunter let Kato take the lead. When they arrived, Kato's uncle greeted him like a son, shouting his praise.

'This is the son of my brother. He is a man. A man to be feared by the Osage or any man who confronts him.' Solemnly Many Wives announced, 'From this day forward, he is to be called No Toe Foot so all will remember what he has done. At his waist he carries the scalp of an Osage who died at the hands of Bird Hunter, the warrior son of Slayer of Enemies.'

A cheer rose from the people. Slayer of Enemies squeezed his son's arm. 'We are proud of you . . . have you slept?'

'Very little. The Osage could have been close behind us, and Kato's foot needed treatment.'

'From this time,' corrected Slayer of Enemies, 'he is No Toe Foot.'

CHAPTER SIX

For the first few weeks after his injury, No Toe Foot had difficulty walking but soon he learned to compensate. Now, almost two years later, only his closest friends were aware of the old wound and a slight limp. Bird Hunter waved to No Toe Foot tending his horses. Most of them were horses they had captured from the Osage. There was much difference between the two men. No Toe Foot displayed almost as much pride in his horses as he did in his pregnant wife, Dataha.

When he entered the woods, Bird Hunter

met Dataha. She walked with both hands under her protruding abdomen in an unmistakable waddle.

'Ah, wife of my friend, you are so beautiful. It pains me that you have no sister who equals you.'

'Bird Hunter, even the forks of your tongue have forks. I am as beautiful as a buffalo cow.'

'You are beautiful. I see you with the eyes of a man. About you there is a glow that also casts beautiful shadows.'

'Why have you not claimed a wife of your own? For a man who is so knowledgeable of beauty, it is a mystery that you have not married.'

'Why is this a mystery? And to whom is it a mystery?'

'All of the women who are eligible speak of their desires to share your bed. The maidens giggle, spill their water jugs, dump their berry baskets on the ground when you pass. Yet you claim none of them.'

'You have a tongue with many prongs also, beautiful Dataha. Let me walk with you. The ground is very rough. Your footing is not as sure as it once was.' Bird Hunter walked beside her back to the village. 'You should have one of the women with you when you come into the woods. There would be much crying if something happened to you.'

'You make it sound as if I am sick ...

which I am not. I'm with child, a perfectly normal thing. My husband does not fear for me because he knows I am hale and hardy.'

'He does fear for you. He has told me many times that he would ride alone among the Osage if anything ever happened to take you away from him. When we were boys, he often spoke of having many wives, but does he? No. He wants no other because he has you.'

Dataha stopped. Bird Hunter turned and looked back at her. There were tears in her eyes. 'Did he say that?'

'Many times. But it is nothing that should bring tears.'

'It is if you are a woman. At times I have wondered why he has not taken another wife. He has enough horses that he could have many. To know that he does not want them because he has me makes me very happy. For this I thank you, friend of my husband. When the time comes, if you feel the same way about a woman, tell her. Promise,' she said girlishly.

'Yes, I promise.'

Tears streaked her face, making him feel uncomfortable. 'If you are all right, I will leave you here.'

Dataha sniffed and nodded her head.

* * *

Sitting on the banks of the river, Bird Hunter

mulled over Dataha's words. For the first time in months, he thought of the Osage girl at the river and hoped the man he had killed was not her brother. The prospect made him grieve for her.

Then he remembered the young widow in the woods and a longing stirred within him. Maybe it was time for him to marry. Drowsy, he stretched out on his back and folded his fingers behind his head.

Suddenly he was awakened by screams from the village. He jumped to his feet, realizing he had been asleep. He ran toward the village.

A brave named Felento was carried to his lodge, his wife running ahead to make a place for her wounded husband. Then Bird Hunter saw three travois. The body of Deoco lay on one of them. His chest was covered by bullet wounds. Crazy Eagle lay on the second travois. Most of his head was torn away, obviously shot with the gun that belched many lead balls at once, called a shotgun by the white man. On the third, Willow, son of Many Wives. Bird Hunter could not remember which of the wives was Willow's mother. All six wives were on their knees crying and tearing their hair.

'Who can tell me what happened?' asked Falcon Man.

Fat Warrior said sadly, 'We were camped beyond the river the white men called Red.

Deoco had killed a deer, a prime buck. We were skinning it and retelling the hunt because we were happy. The son of Many Wives was guarding our camp, but suddenly he ran into the circle of our fire and was shot before he could warn us of anything. Then the enemy rushed us. Crazy Eagle fired at them but their horses trampled him. His aim proved true. One man had an arrow in his shoulder but he did not fall from his horse.

'They fired their guns at us. I could not see how many there were. I was beyond the circle of firelight.'

'Why are you not wounded or dead?' asked Falcon Man.

'I cannot explain what they did or why they did it. When I reached the clearing, they were gone. But they were not soldiers. They were Indians who hunt game for the soldiers and who find their trails.'

'Scouts!' Bird Hunter said scornfully to Falcon Man. 'They are called scouts by the white men. There are Indians among them.'

'Comanche?'

'No. These are Indians that the white man brings from the lands where the sun rises.'

The chief called for Slayer of Enemies. 'Take some men, including your son Bird Hunter, to find the trail of these white men. I will follow with more men. When you have overtaken these men, send your son back to me. Do not attack before I arrive unless you are sure of victory.'

Slayer of Enemies and Bird Hunter raced for their horses. Six men ran behind them. No Toe Foot waited for them at the herd.

'You should stay with your wife, Dataha,' said Slayer of Enemies.

'My wife would think little of me if I did not go to avenge our friends and my cousin.'

'You know your wife best. You may go.' Slayer of Enemies looked at his men. 'We have a fine band here. We can fight the whole army of soldiers. We go.'

He rode at the head of his small band until they arrived at the clearing. The story was there just as Fat Warrior had told it. Hanging in a tree was the carcass of a deer. Crazy Eagle's bow lay on the ground, broken by the hoof of a shod animal.

Slayer of Enemies saw all of this in minutes and was back on his horse following the trail. When the light left the sky and they could no longer see the trail, he assembled them.

'Bird Hunter, go with No Toe Foot. I believe the white men are following a straight course back to their beginning. We can do the same but not blindly. The two of you ride ahead but be on the alert for the white man's Indians. When you know where their camp is and how far, one of you bring me word. The other will stay and watch the camp. Go with caution.'

Riding into the velvet night, Bird Hunter

felt a tightness in his chest. His father had given them a dangerous assignment. Under a full, high moon they sighted the camp but it was not what they expected. There were many soldiers. The horse herd was as large as the one stolen from the Osage.

Lying on their stomachs, they studied the white man's camp. Bird Hunter whispered to No Toe Foot. 'Take my father the news he waits for. I will stay here to watch.'

'Why can I not stay? You return with information for your father.'

'Slayer of Enemies' son should stay.'

Finally No Toe Foot nodded and crawled back to his horse. Bird Hunter did not hear his friend depart. If he could not hear the movements of No Toe Foot at this distance, neither could the men encamped.

* * *

It was almost dawn by the time his father was beside him. 'There are more of them than we expected. I have sent word to Falcon Man.' Looking at the sky, his father judged that Falcon Man would arrive when the sun was high. 'They will be gone by then, but we will follow and watch them. Sleep now, my son. You will need to be rested when the time for their accounting comes.'

Bird Hunter rolled onto his back and quickly fell asleep beside his father.

The sun in his face awakened him.

'I was about to call you,' his father said. 'The whites are getting ready to break camp. We must follow.'

Stealthily, they returned to their horses. Two Comanche braves rode north of the soldiers' trail, Bird Hunter and No Toe Foot followed behind, and the remaining war party trailed south of them.

The taller Bird Hunter rode the roan he had taken from the Osage. His mount was two hands taller than the roan No Toe Foot rode, making Bird Hunter seem like a giant to No Toe Foot when they rode side by side. He seemed so to the Choctaw scout also as he hid in the brush and watched the Comanches.

* * *

From his vantage point on the hill, Slayer of Enemies saw the scout overtake the army detail. The soldier in charge halted the detail to confer with the scout and a soldier who had three stripes on his sleeves. Then a small detachment of soldiers and two of the scout-Indians waited beside the trail while the rest of the soldiers rode off.

When the last of the detail passed, the detachment hid their horses in a gully, concealed their position and waited. They were so well hidden that a rabbit hopped within a few feet of them as Slayer of Enemies watched from above.

'The Indians who travel with the white soldiers are smart like the fox. I would like to take them alive.' He pointed to one of his men. 'You! Ride back and tell my son and No Toe Foot they are headed for an ambush. Be sure to tell them the enemy waits in a gully near a lazy oak tree.'

Slayer of Enemies trembled with anger when he looked back at the gully and the leaning oak tree where water had washed away much of the soil holding its roots. He took three arrows from his quiver and handed them to Fat Warrior. 'Take Whistling Man and climb to the point where water comes from the hills. Follow on foot along the wash until you can see the soldiers. Hide until you hear my call. Then shoot from behind them. Have Whistling Man take extra arrows. Shoot fast and true.'

He felt a pain of anxiety in his chest. Bird Hunter was making a wide circle and would be north of the soldiers now.

'Bird Hunter will attack where the pines rise into the hills,' he told the other warriors. 'Watch the brush for sight of him. When the time is right, we will yell our battle cry from here, but we will circle downward and strike with the sun behind us.'

He was well named, this one. It was an honor to fight at his side. All three Comanches saw Bird Hunter and his followers move into the gully beyond the soldiers. All were ready. It was time.

Mounted. Arrows strung to the bow. Slayer of Enemies lifted his head in a long war cry. He kicked his horse into motion. Staying under cover of the trees, they circled west and galloped at full speed into the clearing. Riders and mounts had been well trained for battle. Dust along the north end of the gully told Slayer of Enemies that Bird Hunter and his followers were attacking. Slayer of Enemies charged in front of them. Behind them Fat Warrior and Whistling Man were raining arrows down on them. The white men fumbled to load single shot Spencer rifles but Slayer of Enemies knew they would be too late. Comanches stormed the position from three sides. Gripping his knife tightly, Slayer of Enemies slammed his fist into the side of a Choctaw's head. The scout went down like a felled tree. Leaping from his horse, the momentum carrying him forward, he knocked a soldier to the ground and buried his knife in the uniformed chest. As Slayer of Enemies rose to his knees with the soldier's rifle, Bird Hunter's war club struck and killed the soldier with stripes on his sleeve.

The fight was over, Slayer of Enemies walked among them. 'Who is injured?' There was no answer. He persisted. 'Who is injured?'

'Stalking Man holds his leg,' Fat Warrior

observed.

Slayer of Enemies examined the leg and found a thorn protruding from the flesh. 'Do you call that an injury?'

'No, Chief, I do not. That is why I did not answer when you asked. I rode too close to a hackberry tree.'

'We have done well, have we not?' asked No Toe Foot.

'We have done well. But I wish you had known we wanted to take the Choctaws alive. Here's one still alive, but not for long. His scalp is yours.'

'This one also lives,' said Whistling Man. A soldier wore an arrow in his shoulder and one in his side. 'My aim was not too good from the gully. Both arrows are mine.'

'Bring their horses. We will take them back to the widow of Deoco. She will enjoy killing them slowly. Many Wives will want to avenge his son and may want the blood of a Choctaw on his own knife. Whistling Man, you may do with that one what you like.'

'I had two chances. I will give him to Many Wives.'

'We must hurry. Their chief will wonder what happened and send scouts to investigate. Maybe they will encounter Falcon Man.'

The wounded men were slung over the saddles of army horses and the small band moved southward. As the ghost light of evening fell, they met Falcon Man.

'Your order was not to attack if we could not win. We could and did. We have no wounds except for the Killer of Hackberry Trees.' When the others learned of his wound, Stalking Man became the butt of much kidding.

Falcon Man saw the collection of weapons taken from the white men. 'We will learn together to use these guns, and we will be stronger, old warrior.'

CHAPTER SEVEN

On the second day, Falcon Man signaled and brought his band to a halt. Two dead horses on the trail revealed that the soldiers knew they were being followed and had pushed their mounts beyond their endurance.

'We must stop. I do not choose to follow them to their beds. We will move south to visit with my old friend, Peta Nocona. He will welcome us, his women will prepare food for us.' Falcon Man and his band swung south.

Bird Hunter rode beside Cicoca. 'I wish we could have overtaken them.'

'We all hoped to better avenge our people, Bird Hunter. But Falcon Man was right not to allow the killing of our horses as the soldiers have done.'

'I know he is right. It was only a wish. But we don't know if we caught the ones who attacked Deoco. Only Felento will know if he recognizes them when they are returned to the village.'

'It grieves me that I was not there with you,' said Cicoca. 'Tell me how your father, Slayer of Enemies, directed the battle.'

Bird Hunter retold the tale of the battle, singing his father's praise.

* * *

When they arrived at the Nocona village, Peta Nocona wrapped Falcon Man in a hug and laughed at sight of his old friend until tears flowed down his dark cheeks. 'It has been a long time, my brother. What brings you here to my fire?'

Around the fire Falcon Man told the story of the recent battle. Peta expressed his heart-felt sympathy for the tears in the lodges of the Kwahadies. Falcon Man could not avoid the bold stares of a white woman who brought roasted antelope to them.

'Who is the white woman that stares at me?'

'My wife, Cynthia Ann. I have a son you have not seen.' He ordered the boy brought to him. Holding the baby high over his head, he said, 'This is my son, Quanah. He is the image of his father, don't you think?'

'No baby should be so homely, old friend. He has his own looks and will some day be a great warrior like his father. There the resemblance ends.'

Peta Nocona laughed. 'You are right.' His wife took the baby, watching Falcon Man. 'Forgive Cynthia Ann. She stares again. She has not completely forgotten the ways of her people and sometimes is too forward.'

'Why have you taken a white woman? No one hated the whites more than you.'

'On winter nights when the cold winds blow, white skin is as warm in my robes as red. In the dark of night a man can not tell the color of the thighs around him.' He roared with laughter. 'There is another white woman among our people. I captured her when the grass was green. She will soon be old enough to marry. You can have her for two horses.'

He called for the girl. Cynthia Ann pushed forward a white girl of about thirteen and stood beside her in the circle of men.

'She is called Shanda. What do you think of her?'

Falcon Man looked at the terrified girl in her dirty, blue gingham dress and turned to Bird Hunter sitting on his left. 'I would like to have her for Bird Hunter, one of my bravest warriors.' He told Peta Nocona some of Bird Hunter's exploits.

'Such a man should be rewarded.'

'Bird Hunter could be called many things grander if he chose.'

The Nocona chief's eyes sparkled. 'Bird Hunter, take the girl as a gift from your chief's old friend. When the Moon of the Falling Leaves is on us and the north winds blow cold, she will be ripe for bedding and you will welcome her to your lodge.'

Bird Hunter did not know what to say. He could not refuse the gift without offending Peta Nocona. 'Thank you. I have no words to express my appreciation.'

'You can name the first son after me. No ... name the first son after your father, who is a brave warrior. Name the second one after me.'

In the morning when they departed the village of Peta Nocona, Bird Hunter rode with the white girl in front of him on the roan.

'So you have taken a wife at last, Bird Hunter,' his comrades teased. 'She is very pale.'

Their laughter sent waves of trembling through her. She tried to avoid touching Bird Hunter. He was the owner of a slave they would expect him to take to his bed in a few moons. Suddenly he had a cure for his problem and hers. He would take her to Swede. He and his new wife could care for the girl or return her to her family.

He talked to her softly. 'Have no fear. I

will take care of you. I will take you to Swede. He will know what to do.'

When they stopped to make their noon camp, Shanda sat on the ground near him. Bird Hunter glimpsed her thighs above the hem of the gingham dress. He would have to marry soon. A wife might change the thoughts and feelings he had when he saw a beautiful girl. Since No Toe Foot married, he no longer talked constantly of women or openly longed for them. Maybe a wife would do the same for him.

Finishing his jerky, he lifted her to the back of his horse. She smiled ever so slightly, for the first time.

By mid-afternoon she slumped forward and slept. Her small breasts, pressed against his back, disturbed him at first. Then he grew accustomed to the feel of her and was more at ease.

'She sleeps. That is a good sign,' Falcon Man said dropping back to ride beside him. 'One who is frightened can not sleep. She will be all right, this one.'

They rode in silence until the chief spoke again. 'What do you plan to do with her?'

'Is it expected that I will marry her?'

'Only if it is your desire. You can take her to your bed for a while but you do not have to marry her. It can be whatever you wish.'

'I would like to take her to the white man who is my medicine.' When the chief nodded approval, Bird Hunter said eagerly, 'His wife could care for her or return her to her family.'

'A good thought. If my daughter should fall into the hands of a white man, I hope he would do the same. I like the way you think, Bird Hunter. When we get back to our village, you can rest and then take her to the white man's ranch.'

Shanda awakened with a yawn. Realizing she leaned against him, she sat quickly upright away from his strong body. Her words were like the prairie chicken when she spoke. But the tone of her voice was apologetic.

'I cannot understand your words nor you mine, but have no fear, nothing will harm you.'

* * *

They made their night camp, and she ate ravenously from the food bag Cynthia Ann Parker had prepared for them. Bird Hunter smiled at her and shyly she returned the smile. When she had eaten, she curled up against a gnarled oak tree and was soon asleep. Leaning against a tree near her, he too slept until the hoot of an owl awakened him. Opening his eyes, he saw she too was awake.

Wayon, guarding them while they slept, called softly.

'It is your turn to stand guard but I am not

at all tired if you prefer to sleep.'

'I will stand my guard, Wayon.'

Bird Hunter got to his feet, stretching, and the girl rose beside him. He tried to make her understand that she could stay and sleep, but she followed him when he took his position in the high cranny overlooking the camp. When he sat down, she sat beside him.

'I wish I could talk to you. We could learn from each other. Where do you come from? Where were you going? Are your parents alive or dead? My name is Bird Hunter. Bird Hunter!'

In silence, she watched him closely. He realized he could see her face clearly and therefore an enemy could also see them sitting in the moonlight. He pulled her into the shadows. At first she drew back as if not trusting him.

'Come,' he commanded. 'I must get out of the light or we will be seen sitting here.'

The urgency in his voice convinced her to follow. They sat on the ground with a large boulder behind them. He leaned against it while she sat upright until her even breathing told him she was asleep again.

'You tire on the trail, don't you little stranger?' Feeling years older, he spoke to her as if she were a child. At first his mother and father would be shocked when he came back with a white girl. But they would be pleased when he told them his plans. The unmarried girls of his village would think that he intended to marry her and that he thought she was better than an Indian girl. It would be best if he did not stay too long before he went to find Swede.

★ ★ ★

As they entered the village, everyone stared open-mouthed at Shanda. Her body trembled. She was as frightened as they were surprised. He dismounted at the lodge of his parents where his mother came out and kissed him on the cheek. His father stood back and looked at Shanda.

'What have we here? You go hunting scalps and come back with a tiny white rabbit.'

Bird Hunter explained his plan to take her to Swede. All the while she sat as close to him as she could.

'She has learned to like and trust you,' his father observed. 'It will be difficult for you to give her up. I think you are right to leave soon.' He turned teasingly to his wife. 'A woman can become like a horse that you love!'

'He lets his words fall like rain in the river, my husband does, where they will do no good. But he is right. You will become attached to her. Respect begets respect. Her trust in you will affect your feelings.'

'Is that wrong?'

'No, it is not wrong,' his father said. 'But your mother is trying to point out that it is wrong for an Indian and a white woman. Water does not mix with fire.'

'Tomorrow I will leave. Swede told me he would make his home where the two creeks come together at the Red River. I can be there at the time of the high sun the following day. It wll be easier with two horses.'

'Does she ride?' his father asked.

'I don't know. She only speaks the white tongue.'

'I will ask her then.' He held two fingers of one hand so it straddled the other hand in the sign of riding and pointed at her. She nodded. 'There you are,' he said triumphantly. 'She rides. It is simple to talk to anyone if you know how.'

CHAPTER EIGHT

On a hill blanketed with the tiny flowers called bluebells overlooking a house in the valley formed by two creeks, Bird Hunter watched for signs of life. Soon Swede came out of the house onto the porch. Bird Hunter kneed his mount down the slope. The girl followed easily behind him.

The Swede lifted his hand to shade his eyes, moving closer to the door where a rifle hung on a peg inside. It was still too far for Swede to recognize him. He kneed the big grey stallion again until the animal broke into a trot. Shanda's horse followed close behind the grey.

Suddenly Swede waved his hat and ran into the yard. 'We have company, Alfa! It's Bird Hunter.'

The Comanche reined to a halt in the yard at sight of his friend's wife standing in the doorway. She was as blond as he, but much smaller, except for her stomach big with child.

'Bird Hunter, welcome. What have you there?'

'This is Shanda.' Bird Hunter dismounted. 'I have brought her to you. She will tell you how she came to be in the camp of Peta Nocona. We have not been able to talk much.'

'My name is Lars Swensen, and this is my wife Alfa. You are very welcome in our home, Shanda. Our friend here is named Bird Hunter, whom I have known since I first came to this country.'

'I'm glad to meet you, sir. I don't understand what is happening.'

'First, let's eat some of my wife's delicious beans and ham. Then we can get to know each other.' In Comanche he spoke to Bird Hunter. 'Come into the house. We have just had the meat of the pig and beans. Very good.' He took his wife by the hand and led everyone up the steps to the kitchen doorway.

'Bird Hunter, now that you see my wife, Alfa, you know why I was so anxious for her to get here. She is by far the prettiest woman west of the big cities.'

Smiling at Swede's praise, Bird Hunter agreed. 'For a white woman, she is very pretty.'

'Lars, what did he say?' Alfa asked.

'He concedes not that you are the prettiest woman but that you are the prettiest *white* woman.'

Alfa extended her hand to Bird Hunter. He looked at the thin white hand hesitantly. She placed his hand in her own and shook it.

Swede explained, 'That is the way whites greet each other. However, it is a greeting usually reserved more for men than women.'

Bird Hunter hung back as Alfa led the way into the house.

'What is wrong?' asked Swede.

'I have never been in a house like this. Everything is made of wood, even under the feet. And it is very large.'

'By the white man's standard, it is a small house. But it is the only house in this part of Texas with a floor made of wood rather than clay.' He urged Bird Hunter to the table. 'Let's have some dinner.'

Alfa set before them plates filled with beans and ham. Shanda lifted her fork to eat hungrily. Awkwardly Bird Hunter lifted the fork and slowly followed her example.

'What is wrong?' the girl asked.

Lars said, 'He has never eaten with a fork before. He doesn't know our ways just as we don't know his.' Sopping his beans with a chunk of cornbread, he continued, 'And now, young lady, tell us how you came to be in the Comanche Village.'

'Some drifters who were traveling part way with our wagon train killed an Indian. They tied him to a tree to let the Indians know who was boss, they said. Two days later the Indians attacked the train. My brother and his wife were killed first. Our parents died four years ago. My brother had been offered a job by an Oregon fur company and we were on our way to the Oregon Territory.'

'Were the men traveling with you also working for this fur company?'

'I don't think so. They were headed for a place called Brent's Fort.'

Swede told Bird Hunter her story. Then he asked, 'Do you have any family at all, Shanda?'

'No, sir.'

'Bird Hunter wants to leave you here with us so we can help find your family.'

She studied Bird Hunter. 'He has been very kind to me. Doesn't he want me to stay with his people?'

Lars questioned Bird Hunter.

'If she stays with my people, she will have to marry a brave or become a woman of pleasure for all the men. My father has explained that fire and water do not mix. The blood of white and Indian will not mix.'

Swede translated for Shanda.

'I would be very proud, Mr. Swensen, to live with you and Mrs. Swensen, but I don't want to be a problem. I will work hard. I can read and write. And when your time comes, Mrs. Swensen, I know all about the birth of babies.'

Alfa patted her cheek. 'You will be no trouble for us. I need another woman to talk to.' She glanced apologetically at Lars. 'It is very lonesome out here sometimes. I am grateful to Bird Hunter for bringing you to us.'

'We are both glad to have you, Shanda,' Lars added, leaving the table and the dishes for the women to clear.

Pulling out a pipe, he said, 'Tell me, friend, what has happened since I saw you last?'

After hours of talking Bird Hunter grew anxious for the sky above and night sounds. He glanced awkwardly at Shanda and quickly left the house. Lars and the women followed him into the yard.

'Don't wait so long to visit, Bird Hunter. A man, too, gets lonesome for talk with his own kind.'

'But it is not good for your people to know you have a Comanche friend. My people have done many bad things, as yours have. But in the eyes of the whites, these things are much worse by an Indian. I will not visit you often but I will watch and I will listen. No harm will come to you from my people if I can prevent it.'

'Yes, Bird Hunter. We are friends. Man to man we are friends, but our people are enemies. We cannot forget that.'

Bird Hunter smiled. 'It is my wish that you have a boy and many of them. They will be beautiful as your wife is beautiful, and strong of body and heart as you are, my friend.'

Timidly Shanda came forward, and taking Bird Hunter by surprise, she rose to her toes and kissed his cheek. Blushing shyly, she hid behind Alfa. With his hand still on his face where the kiss had fallen, Bird Hunter rode from the yard.

* * *

Lars Swensen smiled broadly. 'It makes a man feel good to have such a friend. Bird Hunter is a rare person.'

'What did he say about me before he left?' Alfa asked.

'What makes you think he spoke of you?'

'I could tell by the way he spoke and the expression in his eyes.'

'He wished that we would have many boys as beautiful as you and strong like me.'

'That was very romantic. I would never have thought of an Indian as a romantic. There is a poetic quality about him. I like him. Yes, I like him very much. You have in him a very good friend.' Alfa placed her arm around Shanda's shoulder and squeezed. 'He was very kind to bring you to us.'

Tears brimmed up in Shanda's eyes. 'Thank you, I will try to be helpful. I promise.'

'Just having you here is helpful. Now . . . let's see what we can do about some clothing for you. You are almost my size. Maybe we can alter some of my dresses for you temporarily. When Lars goes to town, he can bring us some yard goods to make dresses for both of us.'

They walked into the house, leaving Lars alone in the yard. He had not realized that Alfa might be lonely.

He too felt good after his visit with Bird Hunter.

CHAPTER NINE

Bird Hunter did not look back as he rode away from the Swensen Ranch. But there was a sadness in his heart he could not explain. A magpie swooped up in front of him with his long black and white tail trailing gracefully in the wind. At another time Bird Hunter would have watched the bird until it was out of sight, but not today.

The sun had moved from the eastern sky to an overhead position. Against the dark green hill to the north he saw grey smoke, and moving towards him, dust. He looked for a place to take cover. He spotted a row of juniper bushes barely high enough to conceal a horse and kneeling man. Quickly he dismounted and with one hand on his horse's neck, calmed him against the rattle of sabres and pounding hooves.

Barely had he taken cover when the first of the fleeing men came into view. There were five soldiers and one of the Indian scouts. With spur and lash they drove their mounts cruelly. A froth-covered horse stumbled and went down, hurling his rider to the sun-baked ground. The rider lay quiet while his horse thrashed the sage-brush with a broken leg.

Bird Hunter waited, expecting the other soldiers to turn back. But they did not. Sprawled on the ground, the uniformed body still had not moved. Nearby, almost hidden in the dust, was his rifle. Bird Hunter picked it up and brushed away the dirt. What he saw then was not a man but a boy in uniform guardedly watching him. As they looked at each other, the young soldier reached for a revolver at his waist. Bird Hunter lunged quickly and overpowered the boy-soldier. Taking the revolver, he rose, aware of the fright in the childish face. The boy's horse continued to thrash wildly in the brush. Pulling his knife, Bird Hunter approached slowly, talking to him in a soothing voice. When the horse relaxed, Bird Hunter slit its throat, wiped the blade on the brush and replaced the weapon at his side.

Instantly the frightened young soldier jumped to his feet.

'There is a ranch . . . there.' Bird Hunter pointed south. The boy did not understand. Making walking signs with his fingers, Bird Hunter pointed toward the Swensen ranch.

'White people?'

Understanding those words, Bird Hunter nodded. Pointing at the sun almost directly overhead, he made further signs and said uselessly in Comanche, 'Half a day to walk to ranch.'

He took the boy's canteen from his saddle and filled it from his own water bag. Handing it back to the boy, he signaled for him to go. The boy hesitated, looked at his rifle and revolver. Bird Hunter shook his head.

'I will keep these. You go . . . Swede ranch that way.'

When he was satisfied the white boy would continue walking toward the Swensen ranch, he rode off in the direction of the smoke.

CHAPTER TEN

Lars lifted his head to listen. He heard a noise in the yard. Soon there was a knock at the edge of the porch. Holding the lamp overhead, Lars slowly opened the door.

'Who's there?'

'My name is Owen Wilkes, sir. I'm in the U.S. Cavalry.'

'Come forward so I can see you.'

The boy stepped into the circle of light, and Lars opened the door fully. 'Come in, Mr. Wilkes.'

'Thank you, sir,' Wilkes said, sinking into a chair. 'May I have a drink of water, sir? The Indian filled my canteen but I'm afraid I did not use it wisely.'

Alfa poured him a glass of water which he emptied in one long drink. 'Are you hungry? I can warm up the boiled potatoes and veal left over from dinner.'

'Thank you, ma'am. You don't need to warm it up. I could eat anything. I had tack and jerky in my saddle pouch, but, not knowing, the Indian only gave me his water.'

'What Indian gave you water?'

'The one that let me go.' The boy studied Lars' face for a moment then went on. 'We were taking a supply train out of Fort Sill to a detachment down on the Red River when we were attacked by Indians . . . twenty or thirty of them. Lieutenant Drake picked a route between the hills because it was easier than going over them. When we got between the two hills, Indians came pouring down on both sides of us. Lieutenant Drake was the first one killed. He went down with five or six arrows in him.'

The boy gulped, shaky with remembering.

'When the scout, Waylon Flax, made a break for it some of us followed. We rode as hard as we could. My horse broke a leg on a little rise and threw me. When I came to, an Indian was standing over me. I thought I was done for.'

'What did the Indian look like?' Lars asked.

'Young, real big, riding a grey stallion.'

'Bird Hunter.' Alfa and Lars said simultaneously.

At the sound of Bird Hunter's name, Shanda stepped out of the shadows, and the bewildered soldier saw her for the first time.

'You know him?'

'Yes. He is a friend,' Lars replied.

'You have friends among the Comanches? They are blood-thirsty killers, sir.'

'Are you dead? No. All of them are not blood-thirsty killers as Bird Hunter proved.'

'He took my gun and rifle.'

'What would you have done if he had not taken them?'

'Killed him, I guess.'

'Exactly! He took them, yet he did not kill you.'

'Yes, and he gave me water and pointed the way to your ranch. So here I am.' The young man studied them for a moment. 'I did not mean to offend you by saying things against your friend.'

'It is a common mistake white people make about Indians,' Alfa said, pouring him some coffee.

Anxiously Shanda asked, 'Do you think Bird Hunter is all right, Mrs. Swensen?'

Private Wilkes looked from one to the other, confused by their concern for an Indian. He looked into his cup, biting his lip uncertainly until Lars spoke.

'We can put you up for the night. Tomorrow you can go into Buffalo Springs and back to the fort.'

Thoughtfully he pulled a blanket from a drawer. 'It is strange that the scout, Flax, should run. He may be more responsible for your being in a trap than your lieutenant. When you make your report mention that possibility. It doesn't seem quite right for your dead commander to take all the blame.'

'Yes, sir, I surely will. I appreciate your help. I would still be wandering around out there if it weren't for you and your Indian friend.'

Handing the young cavalry man the

blanket, Lars said, 'We are a little cramped for room in the house, Mr. Wilkes. I hope you don't mind sleeping in the barn.'

'No, sir, I don't mind. I would feel much better, though, if you called me Owen. It makes me feel strange when you call me *Mister*.'

Lars smiled. 'Let me know when you are ready to turn in.'

'If you don't mind, sir, I'm ready right now. The ambush and all that walking ... I'm tuckered.'

Returning from the barn, Lars sat silently at the table and stared at the lamp, ignoring the coffee Alfa had poured for him.

'You haven't even touched your coffee. Are you concerned about Bird Hunter?' Alfa asked, bringing her sewing to the table to be near him.

'I'm concerned about Bird Hunter, and about you, and Shanda, and our baby. I'm concerned about the future. The white man came to build a new and better country. But we take what the Indians had in order to build that country. We take it, not share it.'

He paused and she reheated his cold coffee.

'What are we going to build? Another London? Another New York? Or Stockholm? With dirt and waste in the streets, where a man must carry a gun and women are not safe at anytime.' He sighed, deeply troubled.

She placed her hand on his shoulder. 'As

long as there are men like you and Bird Hunter, this country will be all right,' Alfa said soothingly.

Motioning for Shanda to stand on a chair, Alfa fitted the dress to the girl's thin but promising shape.

'What do you think, Lars?' she asked, studying her handiwork.

Lars looked up at the girl. 'My ... my! Bird Hunter has brought us a stealer-of-hearts, that's what he's done.'

'You are making her blush. Does that mean you like the dress?'

'Yes, my dear. I will be escorting Private Wilkes to town tomorrow. Would you like to come with me so you can pick out some more material for dresses?'

With her hand on her stomach, Alfa smiled. 'I think we can make do for a few more months. I want to be able to wear the dresses we will make. We'll be able to wear reds and yellows then. Won't we, Shanda?'

'Yes ... yes, ma'am, we will.'

CHAPTER ELEVEN

When Bird Hunter arrived at the source of the smoke, he found military wagons still smoldering. The first person he saw was No Toe Foot, who sat like a conqueror on the seat of a partially burned wagon. The destruction was almost total. Eight soldiers lay dead, their mounts already herded with the Indians' ponies ready for the return to the village.

'What has happened?' Bird Hunter rode up beside No Toe Foot's wagon.

'The Indian scout we captured told us there were supplies going to a new fort built south of the Red River. Some of the soldiers escaped but we will destroy the new fort before they build it up more. I am glad you have returned in time to ride with us.'

'We are going from here?'

'Yes. Look in this wagon. We have guns, powder, and lead for bullets. Your father can teach us how to use them. It will not be arrows and knives that will kill them, but their own guns!'

Slayer of Enemies rode up behind him. 'My son, you have returned. It is good. We will fight side by side. They will sing around the fires that we are of the same blood, and your mother will be twice proud.'

'Yes, she will.' Bird Hunter was caught up in the fervor of a battle yet to come.

'Are you ready, No Toe Foot?'

'Yes, chief.'

'Then we go.'

No Toe Foot slapped the reins across the flanks of the four-horse team. The wagon lurched into motion as the spanking team swung into a trot. Behind the wagon, heavily armed men laughed heartily at first but finally rode in ominous silence. They had been on the trail less than an hour when a band of braves from the camp of Peta Nocona joined them. They numbered more than those under Slayer of Enemies.

Shortly after dawn on the following day a band of Kiowa under Satanta met them, and a small council was called. A blanket was spread for Satanta and the war chiefs of the bands formed a circle to hear his words.

Bird Hunter and No Toe Foot sat outside the circle and listened. His voice and his words would have been strong had he talked in the softest whisper.

'My friends, the Comanches, have asked that we join them for their fight against the white soldiers. I say it is their fight because it is their land which has been invaded. But their fight is the fight of Kiowa and the northern tribes of Cheyenne, Arapahoe, and Cut throats called Sioux by the French. It is the fight of all men who are called Indians.'

No Toe Foot leaned close to Bird Hunter and whispered, 'He is a great and wise chief.'

Bird Hunter nodded, listening intently.

'All people, Indians, white men, soldiers, Comanches, Kiowas ... We all empty bladders in the same way. We all get our children in the same way. Yet there is a difference. The white men lust to own land.'

He scooped up a hand full of dirt and let it sift through his fingers. 'If the white man would lust for my wife or my daughter or my horse, I could understand. I could fight him for his life or mine. But he doesn't want things we can get more of. He wants the only thing we can never replace . . . our land. We will fight your fight, Comanches.'

Slayer of Enemies paced around the circle of listeners and returned to the center. His voice was so low Bird Hunter had to lean forward to hear. 'Satanta has spoken the truth because it is his way. Now we, the chiefs of the Comanche, must speak. I, Slayer of Enemies, feel we should follow the great Satanta. His people cry when ours are sick. When the buffalo leaves our dry lands for want of water, do we not hunt Satanta's lands? I will follow Satanta proudly. I have spoken.'

When Slayer of Enemies sat down, each of the Comanche war chiefs rose in turn.

'I follow Satanta.'

'And I.'

The meeting was over. Satanta took his place at the head of more than one hundred warriors with Slayer of Enemies at his right hand.

When the sun was still visible in a thin line on the western sky, they made camp for the night. Soon the Texas evening was still and the Red River spoke louder than the men.

There were no fires. They were too close to the new fort. Scouts returning to report to the circle of chiefs were the only movement.

'When I can sit in the circle of chiefs, my food will go down more easily,' No Toe Foot said, as he watched a second scout report his findings. 'Not knowing is worse than waiting for a baby to come. I have not had time to tell you, Bird Hunter. I am a father. Dataha has given me a son.'

'I hope he looks like Dataha. Our people cannot stand another who looks like you.'

'Yes, a tribe is only entitled to one as handsome as me!'

As their banter continued, the last scout returned.

No Toe Foot said, 'I wonder what he has to report?'

'Why don't you go over and tell Satanta to keep you better informed?' Bird Hunter teased as he nudged a Kiowa squatting next to him.

The Kiowa laughed. 'He will no doubt tell you his plans before he hoists you by your heels over a slow fire.'

'He would not do that. He is a kind man.'

The Kiowa's expression turned serious. 'Yes, he is a kind man. When there is need, he cries louder than all the rest. But he also fights harder than all others. There will never be a white man singing the tune he dances to. When these times are gone and we are all forgotten, he will not be forgotten.'

CHAPTER TWELVE

High above the fort, the warparty could see most of the enclosure. Lying in a valley of sun-parched land, the fort was very vulnerable. It bristled with activity. A log wagon departed the enclosure. With it were wood cutters escorted by guards. Satanta dispatched a small band of men to attack the wood detail. 'Wait,' he ordered, 'until there is the sound of our battle, before you attack.'

Among those sent to kill the wood detail was Bird Hunter. He rode down the hillside past Slayer of Enemies. 'I will be careful,' Bird Hunter said softly. A smile showed only in his father's eyes; the old face remained solemn.

A Kiowa with countless scars on his body led Bird Hunter's party. Skillfully he picked footing for his mount, which they followed, where grass lay and no dust rose.

The target of the white men was a stand of young oaks where they had already cut much timber. There were many stumps and small trees on the ground. The Indians took a wide course. They would enter the stand of oaks from the far side and would have them for protection while the whites would have only downed trees and the skeleton of a log wagon. The scarred Kiowa was a formidable foe. Most of the enemies who had left marks on him were skilled but now dead.

The small band took cover in the oak trees, and when they heard the first sounds of battle filtering through the foliage, their Kiowa leader sang the war cry.

As his lance entered the chest of the soldier nearest him, Bird Hunter felt the blast of gun powder along his leg. After the thrust his lance was broken and worthless. He drew the knife at his waist, using the grey stallion to charge the sergeant's horse. Their mounts went down in a flurry of hooves. The sergeant's back arched across a felled tree. Raising his knife, Bird Hunter was prepared to plunge it into the blue coat when he realized there was no fight left in his opponent. Both arms were spread wide. In the right hand a revolver hung loosely, but the sergeant could not lift his arms. Bird Hunter took the weapon from the almost lifeless hand. There was a helplessness in the pale blue eyes but no fear.

The fight was over. All were dead except the sergeant and a lone wood cutter who had raced for the fort.

The Kiowa leader examined the soldier draped across the log. 'Aren't you going to kill this man?'

'He is worse than dead. He cannot move

. . . except for his eyes.'

'His scalp is yours if you choose to take it.'

Like a ghost, the sergeant spoke. 'What . . . are you . . . waiting for?'

'One muscle still works,' the Kiowa said. 'Do what you will and let us join our brothers at the fort.'

All of the Kiowa were mounted except for Shumsa, who leaned against an oak tree, his hand over a wound in his stomach.

'We go now to the fort,' said the scarred Kiowa. 'We will return for Shumsa. He cannot fight more today.'

Bird Hunter checked the stallion for injuries and mounted. Glancing back only once at the paralyzed sergeant, he rode after the others.

Black smoke billowed from the fort and told the story against the blue sky. Bird Hunter looked at each fallen body as he rode past, fearful that he would find No Toe Foot or his father. They were not there. Inside the gate, most of the dead soldiers had not even gained the wall before they were killed. Satanta had done well in his surprise. Beyond the center of the fort, No Toe Foot knelt beside a quiet form.

'It is Slayer of Enemies,' his friend said simply.

Bird Hunter slipped hurriedly to the ground and knelt beside his father. 'How bad is his wound?'

'He will live but he will not be able to ride. The wound is very bad.'

'There are two wounds,' Bird Hunter said.

His father opened his eyes. 'My son. I am so glad to see you. Are you hurt?'

'No, Father. But No Toe Foot thinks you should not ride. How do you feel?'

'Only my back pains me.'

'A wound in the back as well?'

No Toe Foot said, 'There is much skin taken from his back. He slipped along the ground when he was unhorsed and it tore off the skin. We will have...'

Suddenly a Kiowa lookout shouted. 'Many soldiers come! Many soldiers!' he called.

'Help me get on my horse.'

'His life will flow out of him if he rides,' No Toe Foot protested feebly.

'I can't leave him here. The soldiers will hang him.'

No Toe Foot helped Bird Hunter lift Slayer of Enemies onto his horse. Blood streamed from the wounds in his side and shoulder.

'I will keep this place to our back so we cannot be seen. With the fort between us the soldiers will not see us before we make good our escape. I will ride slowly so he will not fall. Is it your plan, Satanta, to run?'

'Yes, there are more than we number. They will arrive before the sun is overhead. They have many guns.' He paused. 'How is my old friend?'

'My son will take care of me. Don't wait for me. It is better that you run so you can fight again tomorrow.'

'We know that, you and I. Help your son and his friend to understand. Now I must go. Come with care at a safe speed. There are yet many pipes to smoke and sons to be made!'

'Pipes make me cough. Making sons does not!'

Satanta laughed and rode away to rally his men. Bird Hunter saw the soldiers' women crying over the bodies of their men. There would be keening in his village too when they returned. He hoped his mother would not be one of them.

No Toe Foot rode behind Slayer of Enemies to keep him on his horse.

Bird Hunter called back to his long-time friend. 'You are a father now and have much to teach your son. Go with the others. I will ride slowly so the whites will not see my dust.'

'The route you follow will take you away from our fires. You will have far to travel before you can turn back, and there is much danger.'

'But the soldiers will follow the larger number. Perhaps they will not even come my way.'

They had ridden beyond the stand of young oaks, past the sergeant who lay waiting still for someone to rescue him.

Bird Hunter stopped so his father could rest.

'How are you, Father?'

'They use painless bullets, these soldiers.' He tried to smile at his own joke.

'Can you still not feel them?'

'No.'

'There is very little bleeding.'

Behind them, No Toe Foot rode below the crest of a range of brushy hills. His horse loped smoothly, eating up the distance between them rapidly. When he had overtaken them, No Toe Foot dismounted and smiled reassuringly. 'They do not follow. When do you plan to circle back?'

'When it is full dark, so we are safe when there are no hills or trees for us to hide behind.'

His father spoke. 'You do well, my son. You speak with wisdom beyond your years.'

'Thank you, Father. Do you think you can eat? Or drink water?'

'Yes, water. I am not hungry. I am beginning to feel the wounds.' His face seemed drawn and much older.

After he had finished drinking water, he wanted to dismount. 'The horse needs to rest. It will be good for me to walk for awhile.'

Together they helped Slayer of Enemies to the ground. His first steps were slow and cautious until he began to regain his strength. With short strides he walked beside his horse for over a mile.

'Are you tired?' No Toe Foot asked.

'I am fine, No Toe Foot. Soon you can help me sit my horse again, but I will walk as long as I can so the animal will not give out.'

Throughout the moonless night they traveled eastward. Shortly after sunup, they saw dust to the south. No Toe Foot rode to investigate. Soon he returned. 'There are soldiers led by an Indian-scout. They come fast. They could have guessed what we are doing.'

For a short distance they loped. Each jar brought new traces of blood to Slayer of Enemies' wounds. They stopped.

Bird Hunter said, 'You go with my father. I will ride back to mislead them.'

'Now you do not speak with wisdom,' his father argued. 'Ahead is a small stand of Apache plume. I can hide there. We will hope the scout does not read the sign and notice one of the horses is riderless. It is a chance we will have to take. When you have lost them, come back for me.'

'If they find you, they will hang you to one of the trees.'

'You do not have a choice. I cannot ride. You cannot stand against so many. Go while there is time for me to get well-hidden. I am your war chief as well as your father and it is an order!'

* * *

Bird Hunter anxiously looked back to the Apache plume where his father lay hidden. No Toe Foot dropped back beside his friend. 'We can find a place to wait to be sure they pass him by. Have no fear for me. My life is yours when it is needed, just as yours would be mine. If they find him we will attack fiercely and kill many white men before we are killed.'

'You are a true friend, Kato.' Unconsciously, he lapsed back to his friend's boyhood name. 'But Slayer of Enemies has given us an order, and we will obey our war chief.'

All day they rode and the soldiers' dust followed. But in the fading rays of light, their dust turned south again on a course back to the fort. From the top of a hill, No Toe Foot studied the trail behind them. Hills to the west seemed to hump their backs to the last fading warmth of sun, as he returned to Bird Hunter.

'I think they have given up. We can go back to Slayer of Enemies.' With a sigh of relief, Bird Hunter wheeled and they galloped westward. The moon was high when they reached the Apache plume. They called softly to the old man.

'He is here!' No Toe Foot knelt over the unconscious form. His body was cold but there was shallow breathing. 'He lives!' No Toe Foot said jubilantly.

They cut poles for a travois and lifted him carefully. They were three days of hard travel from their village.

'But we are no more than a day and a night from the home of your friend.'

'Swede?'

'Yes, although he may not help us. He surely knows now of the many dead we left at the fort. It could make a difference in his feelings toward us since he is white, and those we killed were white.'

'I think he would want to help no matter what the color of our skin. It is his way. We will try. When we near the two creeks, you can ride ahead and tell him what has happened.'

CHAPTER THIRTEEN

They were struggling along Buffalo Creek. It was time for No Toe Foot to ride ahead. The moon was high and an owl called in the distance. Bird Hunter led the horses. His father's horse had stumbled twice, knees buckling. They had traveled all day and into the night without stopping for food or water. If they were overtaken by soldiers now, he would not have enough strength left to fight.

He had lost track of how long No Toe Foot had been gone when he heard the rumble of a white man's wagon. Suddenly the vehicle loomed ahead.

No Toe Foot rode one of Swede's horses. Swede drove a wagon piled with buffalo robes.

'Friend Bird Hunter, how is your father? Alfa is getting ready for us. He will ride easier in the wagon.'

They transferred Slayer of Enemies to the comfort of the buffalo robes. No Toe Foot would stay to rest and feed the horses. 'Have no fear for me. I will remain here and sleep, as quiet as a mouse in a maize sack.'

'I will look for you and the horses in one day.'

No Toe Foot watched his friend and the wagon out of sight, lost in the silent darkness. Bird Hunter left the grey stallion behind and rode Swede's horse.

There was no need for No Toe Foot to picket the tired animals. Contentedly they grazed as he sat against a large beech tree, drawing his blanket about him to sleep.

At the Swensen ranch, Alfa and Shanda were waiting for them in the yard when they arrived. Quickly Alfa felt the wounded man's face.

'He is feverish, Lars. Take him into the house where I have fixed a bed for him near the fire. Shanda will see that Bird Hunter has food and a blanket for the barn.'

When he had eaten, Shanda took Bird Hunter to the barn where a ladder led into the hay loft. It took his remaining energy to make the climb. He sank into the blankets piled for him there and in seconds was asleep, knowing his father was in good hands.

* * *

Shanda leaned over him and shook his shoulder. 'Bird Hunter . . . Bird Hunter,' she whispered. Instinctively he rose with knife in hand. But she was not afraid and motioned for him to follow. He had slept most of the day. His legs were stiff from the long ride and the long sleep. The sun was low in the sky and he squinted as he walked behind the girl to the house.

Alfa greeted him at the back door with a cup of hot milk. The cup shook in his hand from fatigue and hunger. Alfa motioned him toward the table. She placed before him a dish of broth, with chunks of beef and vegetables.

Swede encouraged him. 'That is good for you. It is called soup.'

'How is my father?'

'He has eaten. The fever is broken and he sleeps. I tied him to the bed so he does not hurt himself when he sees us.' He refilled Bird Hunter's glass. 'Since you haven't told him about us, it is best. The bindings do not hurt him.'

When the sun was high the next day, No Toe Foot arrived, with their horses and bad news. 'There are soldiers checking ranches and farms for Indian raids. I have watched them since the first rays of sun. They will come here.'

'I will ride out to meet them so they won't come to the house,' Swede said. 'You need to eat now, No Toe Foot. There is plenty of food on the table.'

No Toe Foot balked at the door, as Bird Hunter had first balked. There was freedom in a tipi of buffalo hides. A house of wood made him feel like he was caught in a rabbit snare. Neither did he understand the ways of the knife and fork. Finally seated uneasily at the table, he studied Bird Hunter awkwardly, using a fork.

Alfa called to him. 'Bird Hunter, come quickly!'

He rushed to the pallet where his father lay straining at the bindings.

'Father, these are my friends. You are in the home of the white man who is my medicine. This is his wife, who will help you if you will let her. When I take away the bindings you are not to fight or get up until she says you may.' Bird Hunter drew Alfa to the bed where his father could see her. 'She will say when you are well.'

Slayer of Enemies nodded weakly, and his son removed the ropes. There were bandages around his chest and waist. In a pan beside the bed were two bullets.

'Here are the white soldier's bullets Alfa has taken from your body. You can wear them about your neck and tell of them around the fires when you are well.'

'I am well enough to travel. Your mother will worry and cry for us.' He was weak with the effort to talk. 'She will think we are lying dead,' he gasped. 'A woman needs to know. I must go so she can see that I am not dead.'

'You cannot travel. I can go or No Toe Foot can go to tell her what has happened.'

'Both of you should go. No Toe Foot has a wife who carries and needs to know he is not dead.' He rested only a moment. 'Our village will need the protection of many braves now. The soldiers will attack our women and children. It will not be known anywhere but at our own fires that we did not kill women and children.' He lapsed into silence, exhausted, and slept again.

Bird Hunter returned to the kitchen and found No Toe Foot mastering the fork. He had eaten most of the food Alfa had set before him. Alfa looked pleased.

'I have pie too.'

They looked at her quizzically. From the warming oven she took an apple pie and cut a piece for each of them.

* * *

Lars Swensen rode to meet the detachment of soldiers beyond Cypress Creek. Flat against the back of the house Bird Hunter and No Toe Foot waited. As the soldiers rode away, the Swede waved and watched them go. Feigning indifference, he rode casually back to the house.

They met at the barn. 'They're riled good! Twenty-eight soldiers and four Indian scouts were killed at the fort. The Lieutenant admits it was in retaliation against the army, but it's still his duty to find the Indians who were there.'

With bitterness No Toe Foot replied, 'It makes no difference to them. They attack and kill villages of women and children. And the helpless ones. There are no men among them who will face the braves.'

'Our being here will cause danger for you, Swede. No Toe Foot and I will leave. When the sun has set four times, we will be back for my father. He can not ride now.' As Bird Hunter prepared to leave, Shanda was watching. He smiled at her.

'Tell her she looks better than when she was with my people.'

She blushed at Swede's translation and ran shyly into the house.

CHAPTER FOURTEEN

Bird Hunter plodded tired and hungry into his village. His mother met him with great relief, looking past him for his father.

'He is being tended by the wife of my white friend.'

'What are his wounds?'

When he described them, she studied his face. 'Does this white woman know the ways of tending a man's wounds?'

'Yes, Mother.'

'Will she sing him to sleep when the fires from the wound race through him?'

'That is not their way. They have other means of treating fever.'

Taking her gently by the elbow, he led her to the circle of tipis.

A Kiowa came to meet him.

'I am Natuk. My chief Satanta asked me to bring word of his friend, Slayer of Enemies. Does he live?'

'A white man and his wife are taking care of him.'

'Satanta will be interested to hear of this. It is strange that, after we killed so many of them, a white man tends a chief who killed not less than three of them.'

'Tell your chief that I, Bird Hunter, the son of Slayer of Enemies, am pleased that he is so concerned for my father's welfare. When he needs me or my friends, we will gladly come.'

'I will tell him. He has already said the son of his friend is a brave and gallant warrior.'

Natuk rode off eagerly with the good news for his chief. On the ridge of the first hill north, he waved farewell to his Comanche friends.

* * *

When Bird Hunter reached the Swensen ranch, his father walked stiffly to meet him.

'Why are you walking? Did Alfa say you could walk?'

'She said I could not. But women do not understand. A man must walk, he must run, he must ride as soon as the wounds are healing or he will become old before his time. If a man listens to a woman, she will have him eating soup and broth for the rest of his life.'

'There are many things a woman knows more about than a man. The treating of wounds is one of them. Can you ride?'

'I am ready now to attack the big fort called Sill.' He laughed but Bird Hunter could see the pain it caused him.

'I see you brought a squaw's horse for me. How can I ride into the presence of my people on a horse like that? This one has not had more than one foot off the ground at one time in all her life.'

'Take this one or you will wait for the setting of four more suns.'

'I am your father. You cannot tell me such things.'

'These are the orders of my mother!'

Alfa and Shanda came from the house to greet him. 'Where is Swede?' Bird Hunter asked.

'He took the wagon for provisions,' his father replied.

Bird Hunter shook Alfa's hand when she offered it. 'I cannot talk to her. We do not understand the same tongue. If I could just make her understand we have a full day to travel. I can smile until my face is sore, but we have understood nothing when it is over.'

Slayer of Enemies made the sign of two on horse back and pointed to his son and himself. Then he made the sign that they would ride away to their village. Alfa watched intently, then shook her head and pointed at his wounds.

'She understands and says I am too sick. This is the way of women. They will never believe a man's wounds are healed enough for him to go the way of men.' He flexed the muscles of his chest to show he was well enough to travel. 'When we are back at our own fires, your mother will worry and tend me until I feel like a helpless old man.'

'It is their way.'

‘But that does not mean I must be pleased by it. Come, we go.’

Again Slayer of Enemies made the sign that they would travel. Alfa gave up arguing. With his eyes Bird Hunter said goodbye to Shanda. Unhappily, she lowered her eyes and looked at the ground.

★ ★ ★

They had traveled a day from the Swensen ranch when soldiers appeared from the east. There were a great many of them and two wagon guns the whites called cannons. Silently Bird Hunter and his father sought the cover of a grove of scrub oaks. The column of whites passed.

‘We cannot fight against such weapons,’ his father said sadly. ‘Their wagon guns can kill many of us with each firing. The guns tear a horse apart while he is still ridden.’

‘How can this be? Have you seen one shoot?’

‘No, but Falcon Man has. He saw them fired against the Mexicans. Big balls sail through the air from these guns. The ground roars like thunder, and more men fall than you have fingers. They are bad.’

‘We must hurry to tell Falcon Man. These men and their guns are on the way to the fort we have destroyed. They will build it up again. Soon we will have to tear it down as before.'

'With those guns to defend them, we will not tear it down so easily again.' Slayer of Enemies spurred his mount and rode ahead of his son. The older man sagged silently. Bird Hunter could not tell if it was because of his wounds or the guns.

* * *

The people of their village ran out to meet them. Slayer of Enemies braced himself tall as he rode among the well-wishers. Falcon Man stood with his arms folded across his broad chest.

'Welcome, friend,' he called to Slayer of Enemies. 'We were concerned for you until your son brought news of you. I will save my tears for another day.'

'For many moons, I hope,' Slayer of Enemies said. 'We have shown death our backs, you and I. May we live until the children not yet born are old and grey!'

'When you have said your hellos to your wife and eaten in your own lodge, come to my fire.'

'Yes, Falcon Man, there is much to discuss.'

Slayer of Enemies felt a tug at his sleeve and looked down into the smiling face of his wife. 'You did not cry for me, did you, woman?'

'No. I did not cry. When you left, you said you would return. It has not been your way all these many moons to make false statements.'

'Have you food ready? Twice I felt I would stop and eat this horse. Although she is not very good for a man to ride, she might be good enough to fill a man's stomach.'

Bird Hunter dropped back, allowing his father the glory of return. He saw No Toe Foot beside his wife. Dismounting at his friend's lodge, he said, 'There is much to tell you.'

'About the victory?'

'Much more,' said Bird Hunter. 'We have seen scores of men and cannons going to the fort. Our fights against the whites is like draining the river with your hands. Our victories are like drops against their endless flow.'

No Toe Foot studied his hands. A smile crossed his face like the shadow of a bird on the ground.

'What was your thought?' Bird Hunter asked.

'You would think my head has gone empty if I told you.'

'Tell me anyway.'

'We could steal these guns. At least one of them. Then we could roar like thunder.'

Bird Hunter studied a column of ants at his feet. One of them carried a dead beetle four times his own size. Bird Hunter moved a stick in the path of the ant. Still carrying his burden the tiny creature crawled over the stick and continued on his way.

'We need to be like the ant. They can move but are not easily seen. If they are seen, they are ignored. If we were like them, we could move into the fort and carry off their guns in the middle of the day!'

'Dataha's uncle, Faltar, cannot draw a bow or handle a lance since he lost his arm. He could go to the fort and become a Hang Around the Fort man. Although he has lost his arm, he has not lost his thinking. He can learn the habits of the white men, the best time, and the best way to take the guns,' No Toe Foot proposed.

'There's one problem. Comanches do not become Hang Around the Fort people. The soldiers would become suspicious if a Comanche should sink so low.'

Bird Hunter rose and leaned over Dataha to No Toe Foot's son. 'He is getting stronger and braver. Soon he will be riding with us to hunt the buffalo.'

Dataha drew her son closer to her breast as if to protect him from becoming a man.

A scene from their boyhood flashed through Bird Hunter's mind. 'It would be like our raid on the Osage!'

'But much more rewarding. Shall I talk with Faltar?'

'We will talk to him soon together. First there is something I want to do.'

'What is that?'

'Ride ... with the wind.'

'Alone?'

'I just want to ride. To let my horse go where he will, and I will see what is beyond his head.'

'That is the story of an unhappy man, my friend. You need a wife.' He reached over and patted Dataha's knee. 'A good wife will make you forget all bad things. When you have a dark day, she can chase it all away in your robes at night.'

Dataha lowered her head and blushed but she was pleased with her husband's words.

'No Toe Foot, I want you to ride with me when the sun is new. You will be back by the time the moon is up.'

'Yes, when the sun is new, we will go,' No Toe Foot agreed, a puzzled frown on his face.

CHAPTER FIFTEEN

Bird Hunter sat high on a hill looking down on the village of Peta Nocona. His horse grazed beside him. Suddenly the stallion raised his head and snorted. Bird Hunter calmed him with a hand on his neck. A small band of Osage moved toward the valley of the wild horses.

'They are fools to come so close to the braves of Peta Nocona. He will have their heads on lodge poles before they know he is near.' As if his words were a prediction, a band of Nocona braves swooped down to attack the Osage. They came from out of the sun, riding with full force down the hill. The fight was over instantly. The Osage lay dead, their scalps lifted swiftly.

Bird Hunter mounted his horse and rode down the hill. He called out to them.

'I saw from the hill. My brothers are brave and swift.'

'Why are you here, brother from the south?'

'Just following my horse.' He looked at the slain bodies of the enemy. 'It was foolish of them to venture so far into our lands. They were led by a fool.'

'His route was chosen for him. We led him so he would wander further into our lands. We only killed them now because we had tired of the game and want to get back to our fires.' Another Nocona warrior pointed to scalps at his waist. 'This is what remains of a war party that attacked a Kiowa hunting party where the sun and the earth come together.'

'You killed them all?'

'A few ran north to their own country. But we will get them another day.'

Bird Hunter lifted his hand in parting and rode north.

The braves of Peta Nocona silently watched him ride.

* * *

When he had cooked a fat prairie hen over his small fire, Bird Hunter moved deep into the shadows away from his fire to eat. As the last embers faded, he saw movement beside a large cedar tree growing up through a boulder. Slipping out his knife, Bird Hunter circled with the silence of the evening shadows. He crawled on his stomach along the ground.

From the darkness above, an attacker came down on his back. The assailant was light of weight and with his left hand, he caught the back of the neck. The neck was thin and soft. He hesitated, ready to plunge his knife into the thrashing body beneath him.

'Who are you?'

'You speak Comanche.' It was a woman's voice, breathless and angry.

'I am Comanche. I am Bird Hunter, son of Slayer of Enemies.' He looked up and saw another woman standing threateningly over him with a raised tree limb. 'Put that down! We will talk at my fire.'

A girl with the body of a woman scrambled to her feet when he released her. The two women remained alert to do battle.

'Why are you sneaking around in the dark near my fire?'

'We are Kiowa from the hunting party. We were attacked by the sons of dogs called Osage. They killed everyone except us.' She was again breathless, retelling it. 'She hid in the carcass of the buffalo she was cleaning. I hid in the tall grass that grows in the water. I saw everything.'

'Come to my fire. After you eat, you can tell the story.' He led them into the clearing and stirred the fire to life. Ravenously they ate the cold hen he had left.

'Now tell me what happened.'

'I am Yahanna. Many moons ago my husband was killed by the Osage. This is my daughter Fawna. Latonna had spoken for my daughter. But he was killed when the Osage attacked two suns ago. We help with the skinning and are given robes and meat for the cold moons.'

'Why did you not make your presence known to the braves of Peta Nocona when the Osage were driven off?'

'We heard the fighting but could not tell who had won. It would not be wise to expose ourselves and then find the Osage had won!'

'Both of you sleep in my robe. I will watch over you until it is time to go.'

During the night he kept the fire alive but sat in the shadows so he would see without being seen, except for the girl watching him from the robe. He discovered that her watching disturbed him.

With the first glow of morning light, he built up the fire and went to care for his horse. He heard her behind him.

'He is beautiful. Do you call him by a name?'

'No. He is just my horse. You should not be talking to me. What if your mother hears you?'

'She would not mind. Talking does not rob a woman of her maidenhood.'

'There are some who think so.'

'My mother is not one of them. She has picked a provider for her when we are back with our people. It is her wish that I do the same.'

'Without marriage?'

'So? If I should marry, it would be better. Should I starve if no man will take me for his wife?'

He lapsed into silence.

'Tell me, Bird Hunter. Would you have thought less of your wife if she had not come to you as a maiden? Would you have thought less of her if you had bedded her before the chief made you one?'

'I have no wife.'

'You have no wife? What is wrong? Can you not bed a woman?'

His neck felt hot and red. *Why should he*

have to defend himself? he thought. 'Of course I can bed a woman and have done so! That is not your concern. Only if I planned to bed you should you be interested,' he said sharply. He studied her for a moment. 'Why do you not cry for Latonna?'

'Why should I? I didn't like him. When he ate, he sucked his teeth and made loud noises. He scratched himself when people could see him. He was very rich and already had two wives. He was also very brave, but I didn't like him.'

'Still, you should not be talking to me.'

With a toss of her head, she went back to the clearing. He could hear the two women talking indistinctly as he rubbed his horse with dry grass. When he returned to the fire, the leftover meat was hot and waiting for him. They ate in silence. In the presence of her mother, Fawna kept her head down. When neither of the women were looking, he studied her and liked what he saw. She was very pretty. She was even prettier than Dataha.

Having finished eating, they followed the growth of fir trees and moved westward. By mid-day they passed again near the valley of the wild horses where the Kiowa hunters were attacked. Being far fewer in numbers than the Comanches, the Kiowas were always subject to attack by stronger tribes. Bird Hunter remembered a story his grandfather had told him, that the Comanche had become friends of the Kiowa, and wanted them to become a part of the Comanches but they chose to remain as they were.

Bird Hunter told Yahanna his grandfather's story.

She nodded her head. 'It would have been good. The sons of dogs would be more reluctant to make war on us if we were a part of your people.'

As he talked with Yahanna, Fawna moved ahead of them, and Bird Hunter became aware of the slight rolling of her hips as she walked. Slight, but enough to make a man bump into trees or walk over a cliff!

'There!' Yahanna said with alarm.

Bird Hunter saw dust over the next hill coming from the east. With a sharp eye, he spotted a deep gully at the edge of the woods. Quickly he led them into hiding and forced the horse to its side, motioning for the women to keep the animal quiet. With his bow strung, he fitted an arrow from his quiver to the string.

Creeping forward, he watched until men rode out of the dust.

'Osage!' The girl whispered, with a hiss in her voice.

'Get back out of sight.'

'I am not in sight. But if they come this way you will need help.'

'What can you do?'

'Fight, as I did last night.'

'If that is what you call fighting, you would be better off out of sight.'

'Had I not lost my knife, you would be dead,' she said with a spark of venom in her voice.

'You are right.' He slipped the knife from his waist into her hand. 'Use it well, if you must, but on the Osage!'

'I will.' She moved closer to him. Her thigh rested slightly against his own. Again she disturbed him. When the Osage rode by and were out of sight beyond the hill, he reluctantly moved away from her.

She was smiling up at him. 'I have wondered what it would feel like to be close to a man like you.' She smiled, adding, 'It was good.' Then she rose and walked down the gully to join her mother.

'We will stay here for a while. They are still too close for us to risk making dust.' Taking jerked antelope from his pouch to eat, he sat on the edge of the gully in order to see in all directions. Below him was the girl. From his position he could see down into her dress. He could not keep from looking at her breasts. He was reminded of an Osage girl bathing a very long time ago.

When it was safe, they continued their journey.

Soon they turned north to reach the lands of Little Mountain. His traveling companions were from the main band led by the chief of chiefs.

Walking ahead of the horse and woman, Bird Hunter lifted his hand in warning when he saw riders in the distance.

'I should walk.' Yahanna whispered. 'Our people should not see you walking and me riding.'

'Are you sure these are your people?'

The girl squinted. 'I am sure.'

'How can you be?'

'There is one who rides twisted because he cannot sit a horse like others.'

'Why is that?'

'He is called Broken Hip. He was wounded many moons ago and walks with a limp. As a child I mimicked his walk as did all the other children.'

'You are still a child,' Bird Hunter said as he watched the coming riders.

'Do you always look at the breasts of children?' She smiled knowingly. 'When you sat above me, you could not look away.'

Twice he tried to refute her words. He wanted to lash out at her, but she was right and they both knew it.

Her mother had dismounted and stood close listening to the talk of the young. She put the reins in his hand. 'The men of our people will think less of you for walking while a woman rides.'

'You are sure these are your people?'

'Yes.'

He leaped to the back of his horse. 'I will ride ahead and talk to them. If you are wrong, my spirit will be with you always. You will not cook meat without burning it. The seams you sew will never hold.' Nudging his mount, he rode out to meet them.

CHAPTER SIXTEEN

Bird Hunter sat at the fires of Little Mountain, understanding why he had been chosen to replace Islandman many years ago. Having ridden with Satanta, he knew the Kiowa had chosen their chiefs well, but Little Mountain stood tall among all chiefs of all tribes.

Islandman had been the chief of chiefs of the Kiowa until they were attacked by the Osage. When the Osage rode down on their village, Islandman had not thought of the unprotected women and children of his braves. With the courage of a field mouse he had fled into the hills, leaving behind his own wives and children. The old men of his village stood and fought and died while their cowardly chief shivered in his place of hiding and watched what was happening.

Those who survived told of his flight when the braves returned from their hunt.

Islandman was not killed as many wanted but he was cast from the tribe. No one ever looked at his face again. It was then that Little Mountain became chief of chiefs.

'It is with a happy heart that I learn the Osage met their reward at the hands of Peta Nocona's braves. They are good men, all of them. Because the Osage are raiding so far south and west into our lands, it would not be wise now to send warriors to challenge them.' He turned a log in the fire carefully. 'Had the Noconas not punished the Osage I would have had to send warriors, leaving my people here unprotected. Will you take a message to my friend, Peta Nocona, on your return?'

'It was not my plan to return to my people soon. I ride with the wind.'

'Are you unhappy, Bird Hunter? Men who follow their horse usually are.'

'I don't know. How can one tell?'

'You have a good question. I will think on that.' He shifted the log, which burned quickly. 'When a man is cold, a fire is happiness. If a man has a stone in his moccasin and gets rid of it, he is happy. The man who is truly happy is one who has had six daughters and then sires a son. I would have to stand in your skin to know if you are happy. A man can only know this for himself.

'Since you are not riding anywhere, it will not make you late if you spend time with us. There is a lodge which has had no fires for many moons. Use it. Gamble with our men. Eat the food our women prepare. Learn the ways of our people. It will help the Comanche and the Kiowa.'

Little Mountain lifted his hand and motioned for Yahanna to come forward. 'Take our friend to the lodge that once belonged to Trainer of Horses. Build up his fire. See that he has plenty of food and comforts. Your life you owe to him.'

Yahanna allowed Bird Hunter to walk slightly ahead of her until they were at a lodge painted with many horses.

The lodge was very clean inside. There were many thick robes. Clay pots sitting near the fire pit were clean. The woman built a flawless fire. It burned low and did not overheat the lodge. It was perfect for cooking also without making the occupants uncomfortable.

When he had eaten, Bird Hunter sat drowsily watching light from the fire. A woman entered and closed the flap behind her.

'Fawna?' He sat upright to see her.

'Yes.' She walked around the fire pit and stood before him. She had washed and put on a close-fitting dress to replace the loose sack she had worn since he first saw her.

Standing before him, she reached to her shoulder and untied the thongs holding her dress, allowing it to fall to the ground. Her body reflected light from the fire and set fires in him. He allowed his eyes to trail over her. Her breasts, and the dark triangle excited him beyond endurance.

'Why do you do this?'

'If a woman is to take a man as a provider, it makes no difference if she is not a maiden. What I do is good and will not alter the life I have ahead of me.' She went to him.

* * *

Until time for his departure she shared his robes. During the last night of her stay, when she had drained him of his juices, she lay beside him and ran her hand over his stomach and thighs and chest. As her hand rubbed a path across the muscles of his abdomen, she raised herself on one elbow and looked down at him. 'Did I please you?'

'You have made me understand why I have followed my horse.' She did not understand his meaning, but she did not question him further.

When the sun was a brief rim on the sky, he fed his horse and made ready for the trail. Little Mountain laid a thin hand on the horse's rump. 'We will miss you, Bird Hunter. Where do you go?'

'Back to my people.'

'There is one who wishes to go with you.' He stroked the rump of the horse. 'Fawna, and her mother Yahanna, would like to go with you.'

For a brief moment he stood in front of his horse with the bag of grain forgotten in his hand until the animal nudged him. Hanging the bag around the horse's muzzle, he leaned against a gnarled pine tree. It was true, he desired Fawna . . . but to take a wife?

'What is your wish?' Little Mountain smiled, understanding the plight of the young man.

'I must have time to think. My friend No Toe Foot took a wife as soon as he became acknowledged as a brave, and he seems happy with her. I will think about it and I will talk to you before the sun is high.'

'I will wait for you.'

Deep in thought, Bird Hunter watched Little Mountain depart and was relieved that he had time to think.

Bird Hunter was impressed that the people were so much at ease with the chief of all Kiowa chiefs. He played with the children too. Bird Hunter realized he was witnessing greatness. The Kiowa chief had been revered for saying, 'I have no life. I am an extension of the lives of my people.' Bird Hunter took a walk in the woods and sat with his back against a tree. Soon he fell asleep, and Swede came to him in a dream.

'It is good that you have taken a wife, Bird Hunter,' he said. 'There is only half a man without a wife.' Then there seemed to be a second part of the man, and it was the wife called Alfa.

Bird Hunter awakened troubled by the dream.

He fully expected to see the white man before him when he opened his eyes. The sun glaring down through the trees hurt them. He had made up his mind. He would find Yahanna and tell her he would like to take Fawna as a wife.

* * *

Hers was a pretty face but one he could not read at present. He waited for Yahanna to speak.

Finally she answered, 'I am pleased that you wish Fawna as your wife.'

'You are welcome to come with us back to my people. We welcome you as a member of our lodge as long as you care to remain with us.'

'That pleases me also. It is not my wish to take a man as a provider now.'

'Then it is settled. I will talk to Little Mountain and we will leave when the ceremony is over.'

Bird Hunter felt a new lightness of heart as he sought the lodge of Little Mountain. The chief saw him and smiled. Already he knew why the Comanche came.

'You have chosen well. Fawna will be a good wife. There is none prettier. She works hard. It was not in my heart that she should marry Latonna even though he was brave and no one went hungry in his lodge. He was too old for her, and his bravery would have made her a young widow. You are brave also, but it is better that she marries one like you. The time she has with you will be better.'

The chief squatted beside Bird Hunter. 'What are you going to do about her mother?'

'Take her with us.'

Little Mountain drew a necklace of silver dollars high on his neck. 'There will not be time for Fawna to build a marriage lodge, but there is no need if you plan so soon to return to your people.'

Bird Hunter studied the necklace, remembering the story told. Many moons ago in the white man's year of 1838, the Kiowa attacked a wagon train and captured the silver coins. Some of the older men like the chief wore them at their necks or in their hair. But Kiowas no longer attacked the white man's supply trains as they made their way to a place called Sante Fe.

He was absorbed in his thoughts when the chief spoke.

'The chief of chiefs of the Kiowas gives you this silver dollar from the necklace as a nuptial gift,' he said, obviously pleased with Bird Hunter's decision.

CHAPTER SEVENTEEN

When Bird Hunter neared the top of the hill overlooking the Comanche village near the fork of the river, his wife and her mother rode behind him. Near the circle of lodges, he heard the crying of women. Heel to the flank of his mount, he galloped into the village. There was no sign of an attack, but the wail of bereavement told him there had been a battle. No Toe Foot had been anxious to take the wagon guns from the fort. In his heart he knew his friend had not waited as he had asked.

There was sadness in the faces of his women, who knew too well the sound that greeted them. 'Go,' Fawna said. 'We will follow.'

Bird Hunter forced the stallion into a run. The two mares ridden by the women could not have kept the pace. Dust billowed around him into the circle of tipis as he jumped from his mount. The first to meet him was the one-armed brave, Faltar.

'What happened?'

Everywhere he looked there were women who knelt, crying, in front of their lodges. Faltar finally answered.

'I was sent to the fort to act as a Hang Around the Fort man. I watched soldier movements and when their numbers were low, I brought the information to No Toe Foot. He and the other young men rode out to attack the fort. They killed more than you and I have fingers but some of our warriors were killed.'

'Where is No Toe Foot?'

'Dead.'

'Dead! No Toe Foot is dead?'

'They caught him and hanged him with a rope from the top of the fort wall. He hung outside the fort as a warning for others to see.'

'Why were you not among them? Why do you still live?'

'No Toe Foot did not want me to fight with only one arm. After I delivered the information, he had me return to the fort to be a beggar as before. He felt I could keep acting the role if I had not taken part in the battle. I was sitting along the wall of the fort when they rode down the hill through the entrance where there still is no gate. Many of our young men had guns and attacked before the soldiers could set up the wagon guns to fire.'

'What did they accomplish besides getting killed?'

'They took the wagon guns!' Faltar said proudly. 'One they hurled into the river. The other is beside Falcon Man's lodge!'

Fawna and her mother entered the circle of

tipis.

In front of his parents' lodge, Bird Hunter called. His mother rushed out and put her arms around him.

'If you had been here my son, you might be dead too, she said releasing him reluctantly.

'Did no one try to stop them?'

His father shook his head. 'Had I, Falcon Man, or any of the other chiefs known about this, we would have stopped them. We have lost many of our young men. But they did well! I am not ashamed of what they did!'

His mother scrutinized the two women curiously. 'Who have you brought with you?'

'This is Fawna, my wife, and her mother Yahanna. They are from the lodges of Little Mountain of the Kiowa.' He helped them dismount.

'You are welcome to our lodge. You must be hungry.' His mother led the two women to her cooking fire.

His father placed his hand on his son's shoulder. 'We are so glad you were not here to take part and die perhaps in the foolishly brave battle of your friends. The wagon gun we have is no good to us. We do not have the great balls that shoot from it nor do we have the powder. We could use the powder we have but then we would have none for our other guns. The whites have so much powder and iron balls, they shoot them just to show soldiers how they work. We cannot even shoot once!'

'I will go see Dataha.'

* * *

Dataha was sitting with her son in her arms, rocking him and singing softly. When she saw him, tears streaked her face. He was glad she had not cut her face as many women did when their husbands died.

'It is good that you live, friend of my husband. You would have gone with him to the fort of the white soldiers.'

'They were prompted to do this thing when white soldiers killed the herd watchers and drove off many of our horses.'

'What can I do that will make your sorrow easier?'

'There is no one who can help me bear my sorrow. I must cry for myself. I cannot say I cry for Kato. My tears are for me.'

'My wife and her mother will come to you and help with the baby and the cooking.'

'You have a wife? That is good. Kato often spoke of your unhappiness. He would like to have seen you happy with a wife.'

'I think he would be happy too that you have not cut your beautiful face nor torn your hair.'

'It would serve no purpose.'

CHAPTER EIGHTEEN

Six moons had come and gone. There was unrest among the Comanche people. They were uneasy and mystified that the whites had not attacked.

The time for crying had long passed. Bird Hunter awakened from a sound sleep and lay in the dark listening to Fawna's breathing beside him. It was then, not while he slept, that he had his dream. He sat at the fire pit and watched smoke draw through the hole of his tipi. Swede entered his lodge.

'Bird Hunter. I have come with a message of warning for you and your people. You must leave this place. Soldiers come with the cannon salvaged from the river.'

Having spoken these few words, Swede seemed to turn to smoke and rise through the smoke hole. Bird Hunter sat upright, carelessly pulling the robe from the nude body of Fawna. Half asleep, his wife reached for the robe, awakening to sit up beside him.

'What bothers you?' She yawned. 'Do you not sleep because my love has been too little?'

Gently he drew her to him, her breast pressed softly and warm against him. 'I had a dream.'

'Did it wake you?'

'No. I was awake when I had the dream.'

'That is bad. What is this dream that it would disturb you while you were awake?' Hearing the dream, she drew the robe to her, shivering, but not from the cold. 'Falcon Man must know of this now. You should not wait for him to awaken. Go tell him what you have dreamed.'

He walked through the circle of lodges, pausing briefly in front of Dataha's. He could hear her crying softly. She cried often, even though the time for crying was over. He wondered if Fawna would cry for him in the night. At the lodge of Falcon Man, he could not decide whether to awaken the chief. The old man's voice asked, 'Who is there?'

'Bird Hunter.'

'Wait for me at my fire.'

Bird Hunter waited beside the cold pit a pace in front of the tipi entrance. When the chief appeared from within the tipi, Bird Hunter repeated his dream.

'It was not a dream, young warrior. It was a vision! We will leave this place now. Wake the people. Have them prepare for the trail. No one is to light a fire. We will travel to the land of our friends, the Kiowas. If there is to be a fight, we will have friends at our back that we can trust. Go now.'

While the village prepared for the trail, Bird Hunter sought his father. 'Falcon Man has asked me to lead a band of braves to search out the soldiers and learn their plans.

Will you take care of my wife and her mother? Since they have not traveled much with us, they will not know our ways.'

'Yes, my son. And when you pick your men, do not select only the young and careless. There are older braves among our people who will follow. Pick well the men who stand behind you.'

Many of the lodges were left standing. Hearing of the vision most of the people felt there was little time. Bird Hunter suggested that Fawna help Dataha. Fawna seemed eager to do so.

As he rode at the head of his band, his wife, unsmiling, lifted her hand in farewell.

Faltar rode out to join the departing braves, gripping the reins and a long lance in his only hand.

'Why do you come, Faltar?' Bird Hunter studied the one-armed warrior. 'Our people need you.'

'I am not so old that I stay with the women and children. I can fight as I am needed!'

'My father stays with the village, and he is not helpless.'

'But he is a warrior without question. When No Toe Foot attacked the fort, he left me behind. I have been left behind ever since I lost my arm. No more!' he said stubbornly.

Bird Hunter squeezed Faltar's shoulder. 'You will be beside me. It will be you who protects my back if there is a fight. With you behind me, I will be safe choosing many names for my children, for there will be time for many.'

Picking a trail of heavy grass, they made no dust and rode to save their mounts. Bird Hunter selected a boy from the novice lodge. 'You are small and ride lighter than your elders and will not tire your horse. Ride ahead keeping us barely in sight. You will be the extension of our eyes.'

'You can count on me, Bird Hunter. I have watched and learned. The whites will not see me.'

As the boy rode away, he reminded Bird Hunter of another time when two other boys no older than this one rode into the camp of the Osage and returned with many horses. This one, Little Moccasin, was like the two who had waited on the banks of the river for the Osage camp to go to sleep. Remembering, he ached for the friend who had ridden with him. He swore he would repay the men who treated No Toe Foot like a criminal unworthy of dying like a man.

They made camp but there were no fires. Little Moccasin held his position as their forward eyes. Bird Hunter leaned against a tree and let his mind wander. He thought of Fawna and her warm body next to him. He thought of Swede who had come to him in a vision to warn the Comanche people.

Finally he slept.

Before dawn, he was awake and tending his horse. Faltar sat on the ground working with a narrow strip of buffalo hide.

'What are you doing, Faltar?'

'I am making a harness like the white men use on their horses to lead their wagons. It will fit around my chest. I will fit the back of my lance into it and it will act as a second hand to make the thrust stronger.'

'There is very little chance you will need it. We are here to watch, not to engage them.'

Faltar drew the thongs through his harness with his teeth and smiled at his war chief.

Bird Hunter looked into the sun stretching across the ground. In the distance he could see Little Moccasin. The boy waved. Bird Hunter returned the signal.

'We are ready. Little Moccasin is on the trail.'

Faltar patted the harness on his chest. 'We are ready.'

Heavy clouds covered the mid-day sun. Winds began to blow, bringing with them the smell of rain. As big drops fell, Little Moccasin rode to meet them. Bird Hunter halted.

'They come, but they are far off to the north,' he told Bird Hunter.

'They will cut off the retreat of our people. These scout Indians are wise. They hope to close the door of our escape and prevent us from joining forces with Satanta or Little

Mountain. We cannot allow that. We will pick the battle ground to our advantage.' Bird Hunter studied the land to the north. 'If we meet them in the trees, they will not be able to use their wagon gun.'

Calmly he gave his orders. 'Gather brush to drag behind your mounts. Make dust where the land is free of grass. Make it look like many lodges are moving this way. We wait for them in the trees. If they are fooled by the dust, they will pass through the trees. We will try to lead them without a fight, but if we cannot, we will make a stand where *we* wish.'

He made his way to the stand of scrubby oaks and pines. There was but one path wide enough for the passage of the wagon gun. There he would make his stand. With the horses well hidden he stationed his men among the trees with a clear view of the path.

They waited.

★ ★ ★

Lieutenant Henry Wellington, U.S. Cavalry, was an experienced soldier. He did not commit his men blindly to the woods. He sent four scouts on reconnaissance into the woods. A corporal and one of the eastern Indians rode the trail. A matching pair rode around the outer edge of the woods searching for tracks into the shelter of the trees.

The Comanches had made no effort to

cover their tracks into the trees so the two scouts outside the woods would find them.

In sign language Bird Hunter directed four of his braves to move into position. They would intercept and capture or kill the pair outside the woods. A calm Comanche band waited for the corporal and the scout along the trail. Three of Bird Hunter's band closed in behind them and stole silently along the trail while the remainder of his force cut off escape. Without warning, Little Moccasin jumped into the enemy's path and swirled a robe at their horses. The animals bolted. The corporal was catapulted from his saddle, easy game for Bird Hunter's men. The Indian scout was more difficult to capture. Little Moccasin grabbed the scout by his legs and hurled himself under the horse. The steadfast scout remained on his horse until Faltar rushed him with his lance.

Both men were still alive, giving Bird Hunter the chance to even the score for No Toe Foot. Tying the captives' arms behind them he gave the order to hang them. His men were eager to even the score. They tied a leather thong around each prisoner's neck. Lifting the swaying men high into the trees, they secured the thongs to the base of the tree. Bird Hunter gave the signal.

It was not a good hanging. It was a strangulation. The victors bitterly remembered No Toe Foot's death, seeking some solace in watching the corporal and scout thrash, with their feet high above the ground. The sound of gun-fire brought an end to the short-lived revenge. At the first explosion, the horse-tender quickly brought forward the horses. Bird Hunter led his men out of the trees into the path of two soldiers fleeing to warn their command. Swiftly a flight of arrows brought them down in full view of the column of soldiers. Bird Hunter reined, faced the soldiers, held aloft the rifle taken from the hanged corporal, and shook the air with his war cry.

At the sound of guns, Lieutenant Wellington brought the cannon to bear on the braves reentering the woods. The earth rocked with cannon fire. Bird Hunter halted his men out of sight in the trees. The cannonball whistled overhead, plummeted through the sky, and fell harmlessly deep in the woods.

Braves who had never heard the sound of wagon guns were greatly shaken at first by the intensity. Still they held their horses and waited. Fire balls whistled overhead but fell out of range.

Bird Hunter reassured his braves. 'When the big gun thunders again, they will attack. But we will be here, not deep in the trees, as they think.'

The cannon roared. The soldiers rushed the trees, as Bird Hunter had predicted.

Faltar sat protectively behind his young chief. The pounding hooves echoed in the clearing. Bird Hunter lowered his lance. When the cavalry came within a dozen yards of the trees, Bird Hunter spurred his grey stallion and charged.

The braves broke from the trees and took the military by surprise. There was no time to bring rifles to bear. Shots went wild and lances bore true. Bird Hunter's lance broke in the chest of an Indian scout. He left it, drawing the rifle from the thong at his waist. Wielding it as a war club, he charged again and again. A private on the ground aimed his pistol at the chief's back.

Faltar leaped from his horse and landed heavily on the soldier, whose pistol fired point blank into the brave's stomach. With his knife gripped tightly by his one hand, Faltar, who had refused to be a protector of squaws, stabbed the blade repeatedly into the near-dead private as long as his own life remained. There was no time to recover Faltar's body. Rallying his men, Bird Hunter quickly led them back through the woods to the opposite side.

They circled the grove past the two bodies of the first soldiers killed, and came at the soldiers from their left flank.

At their original position once more, the soldiers were clustered around the wagon gun, waiting.

Bird Hunter halted his men.

'They are ready for us now. We can do no more. We will wait, and they will wait. While they are detained here, they can do no harm to our women and children. We will build small fires in the trees to keep their attention. We will draw the bullets of the wagon gun, if they shoot it. Once the fires are built, retreat from them. When they see our fires, they will know we wait. They cannot move without our attack.'

While they worked, Bird Hunter was finally free to pick up Faltar's body. He would cry a long time for the little man who had saved him from the soldier's bullet.

As the fires began to glow like fireflies in the shadows of the trees, the big gun erupted, splitting trees and throwing dirt and rocks. After each explosion, Bird Hunter's men scrambled forward and rekindled the fires, darting back to safety.

After the third explosion of shell, Bird Hunter led them far beyond range. The white men ceased fire. They too waited.

'How many have we lost?' Bird Hunter asked.

'Brave Faltar and Little Moccasin, who was only injured slightly. You have led us well, son of Slayer of Enemies!'

'Little Moccasin, does your wound pain?'

'Very little, Bird Hunter.'

'You are small but so is the bee that buzzes

around the flowers. From this day on, you can be Little Warrior.'

The boy smiled proudly. 'It is my wish to be as big as you are, Bird Hunter. But if I can not grow so tall, I will become so skilled that you will always choose me to ride with you.'

A grey-haired warrior spoke. 'We would always like to be chosen to ride with you, Bird Hunter.' It was his age that gave so much weight to the tribute, and it pleased Bird Hunter.

'We will leave the body of Faltar here in a shallow hole. Be careful to cover it with rocks so he will be protected. When the soldiers are gone, I will come back and take him to our village.'

A lookout called to Bird Hunter. 'The soldiers have made ready to move their gun. They are getting ready to leave.'

'Let me know which way they travel. If they go toward the path of our women and children, we will attack again when the time and place are right.'

'Yes, chief,' said the lookout before returning to his post.

For the first time Bird Hunter became aware that the men were addressing him as chief.

'How many of the soldiers have we killed?'

Little Warrior held up one hand and three fingers. He also held up a blond scalp. 'When I have my own lodge, this will remind me of this day.'

The grey-haired warrior held up a scalp, a revolver and a bugle belonging to a soldier he had killed.

Quickly Bird Hunter examined the bugle. 'The horn will serve us well. We will learn to make the sound the white soldiers answer to. We will lead them to us or confuse them. It will serve us well.'

For several days they followed the trail of the soldiers. Sometimes they would let themselves be seen and, altering their course, slowly drew the whites away from the route of their people.

On the morning of the fourth day, the two enemies were camped close enough to see one another's camps but not close enough for the firing of the gun.

'It is enough,' Bird Hunter declared. 'We will ride away and pass behind the soldiers where they cannot see. While they wonder where we are, we will go to our people.'

'It is a good plan,' said Little Warrior.

'I need one good man to help me bring back Faltar's body.'

Little Warrior stretched his height valiantly.

'If your wound does not hurt you, come with me, Little Warrior.'

CHAPTER NINETEEN

Fawna shielded her eyes against the sun to see the Comanche band approaching. She did not see Bird Hunter. Her stomach cramped in fear and waves of pain broke over her heart. He was not with them! Tears stung her eyes.

Dataha placed her arm around the shoulders of the Kiowa girl to comfort her.

'He cannot be dead,' Dataha said without conviction.

'They have no drag behind their horses for wounded or dead,' Fawna sobbed.

The grey-haired warrior rode apart from the rest and stopped at Fawna's lodge. 'There will be many songs around our fires about Bird Hunter. He is brave and wise. Without him, we would not have turned the soldiers away.'

'He lives?'

'Yes. He has gone to recover the body of Faltar, who saved his life.'

'Faltar saved his life?' Dataha asked.

'With only one arm he fought like a demon. We will sing of his bravery, too.'

'I must prepare for the return of Faltar, my mother's brother. I will grieve much for him. He was so kind to me when I was small. He would lift me to the back of his horse and lead him until I learned to ride alone. Then he would go with me and watch over me, always fearing that I would be hurt. Yes . . . I will grieve much for him.'

* * *

One morning after two suns had burned their way across the sky and dropped into the night, a lookout galloped into the circle of lodges. 'Bird Hunter comes! With him is Little Warrior.'

Slayer of Enemies and Falcon Man waited together to welcome him. Bird Hunter was not prepared for the welcome he received. The men lifted their weapons and cheered. Women danced and chanted his name.

'I cannot join with you until the body of my friend is cared for.'

'That is the duty of women, my husband.' Fawna stood close beside him. The sight of her made his heart sing. She looked radiant to see him.

Falcon Man and Slayer of Enemies greeted him. Falcon Man spoke. 'I have heard your warriors' praises. It is time for you to sit at the big council fire. From this day on, your voice will be heard as your father's is heard. You will be honored as a chief among chiefs and your words will also be honored.'

A cheer went up from the villagers. And as they had raised their voices, so they lapsed into silence and the honoring of the dead

Faltar began. Later into the night there was singing and dancing. Finally Faltar's body was placed with the arm that had so long awaited him. Again the warrior and his spirit were one.

* * *

When there was work to be done, Little Warrior was always the first to step forward so Chief Bird Hunter could see him. Thus he was chosen to accompany a band to inspect the abandoned village.

'We cannot continue to live like this. Our women must have a chance to build our lodges. We must go after the lodge poles and the hides left behind in our running ahead of the whites.' Falcon Man walked past Bird Hunter and laid his hand on the chest of Eagle Hunting. 'My wish is for information that it is safe for our women to return to the old village. That is all.'

Eagle Hunting was a good warrior and valiant. Many thought he was too brave. He would risk himself and the lives of his followers too lightly. There were shadows of mystery in the face of Eagle Hunting that no one could fathom. Behind the dark mask were thoughts that never came out of his mouth.

Eagle Hunting waved his arm to include the men standing nearest him. 'I will take these men with me.' Among them was the young Little Warrior.

Bird Hunter felt a twinge of sadness to see Little Warrior being chosen for yet another mission. But Little Warrior, wishing to make his name known, was jubilant. Bird Hunter suffered his sadness in silence braced with some small hope.

Beyond the circle of braves stood the father of Little Warrior, Man Who Shivers in the Sun. He too was concerned about his son being chosen to go with Eagle Hunting. There was nothing he could do to change what must come. The test of manhood was inevitable. Stoically, Man Who Shivers in the Sun shuffled back to sit statue-like in front of his lodge.

As the small band trotted away, Shivering Man lifted his hand in half-hearted salute to his son, the excitement in the boy's face tearing at the old man's heart.

Slayer of Enemies sat cross-legged beside his old friend.

'I would not grieve for him too soon,' said Slayer of Enemies. 'He is a wise boy and has promise of becoming a gallant warrior. My son speaks highly of him.'

Shivering Man spoke softly. 'Yes, he is a good boy and shows much promise. If he could follow your son or you, I would not worry. But my son has not had many advantages. I am old, too old to help a young warrior. When you were born I was already a novice. When my son was born my hair was already like the snows of the cold moons. I was too old to have a son. My teeth were but a memory. I had reached the point where birthing daughters was not wise.'

'A baby, any baby is a blessing, Shivering Man.'

'Perhaps not at my age, old friend. My name alone tells the story. Even as a youth, I was hardly stronger than the smallest girls. I could have been called Coughing Man or He Who is Sick a Lot. I was not able to teach him to draw a bow. It was the Teacher of Novices who taught him how to shoot.'

Slayer of Enemies could not comfort him, knowing his words were true.

'Now I must sit and watch him ride away with a man who could bring him back dead,' sighed Man Who Shivers in the Sun. 'Eagle Hunting will return bearing signs of the battle that kills the young men who follow him.'

The old man's words sounded like an omen as the band under Eagle Hunting departed. Their shadow disappeared on the long slope that led the way to the village they had fled.

* * *

Placing his feet high on a sapling oak, Bird Hunter entwined his fingers and placed them behind his head as he lay back on the ground and watched Fawna wash their clothes in the stream.

'Are you happy to be here with my people?'

'I like your people. When I think about it.'

'What does that mean?' His forehead was furrowed with wrinkles.

'I mean it is you I feel for. It is you who makes me happy to be here. If I think of your people, it is prompted by my thoughts of you.'

'No Toe Foot was right. There was a need in me for a woman like you. It saddens me that he did not meet you. He was like a brother to me, and he would have loved you as a sister.'

'Have you thought you would like to have other women?' She asked the fatal female question.

'It has been a thought that I would like all women as my wives. Then I could go for as many moons as I shall live never sharing my robes with the same one a second time.' His laughter was interrupted by a wet shirt thrown expertly at him from the stream.

His laughter ended abruptly when she whispered hoarsely.

'Whites!'

He was instantly on his feet, knife in hand. Three white men sat silently on their horses looking down upon them from the bluffs across the creek. Swiftly Fawna slipped behind Bird Hunter before the white men came close.

In perfect Comanche, the ringleader said, 'I am called Slader. What are you called?'

'Bird Hunter.'

'Mighty funny name for such a big buck. Who is the squaw?' There was an evil air about the man.

'What does it matter?'

'Just being friendly. Didn't mean nothing by it. Can't a man just be friendly with you people?' He shifted in his saddle so his revolver was more readily available. 'Who is the other one?'

Fawna whispered, 'Mother!'

She was close behind her daughter.

'Tell you what I'll do. I'll give you a real fine rifle for them two women folks.' He picked his teeth casually. 'This here rifle is fine. Belonged to the army until I up and left the army. What you say? Want to trade?'

'These are the women of my lodge. They are not for sale or trade.'

'It just ain't right for a man to have two fine pieces like them when we ain't got none. But to show you how fair I am, I'll give you the rifle for either one of them. We ain't hard men to get along with.' The smile on his face said he felt like he had the advantage.

With one hand behind him, Bird Hunter signaled for the two women to run. 'This is the land of the Comanche. You have no business here. I will not trade. You will leave now.'

'Don't get bossy with me, Indian. I'll come down on you like a duck on a june bug and take both squaws.' His hand inched closer to the butt of the revolver. Bird Hunter could hear the women backing away.

'Just don't try to go nowhere, pretty things. This here buck and me is about to come to some kind of terms.' He grinned. 'I have a better offer. Your life for them two. What do you think of that?'

'My lodge pole bears what is left of better men than you who have tried the same.'

The riders who had been left on top of the hill were gradually closing in, taking positions on either side of Slader.

Out of the corner of his eye, Bird Hunter saw Yahanna wade into the stream. She lifted her skirts distracting the white men. Bird Hunter took advantage of the opportunity. His knife plunged into the chest of Slader. Bird Hunter gave a war cry, leaping upon the second intruder, bringing him to the ground.

The horse reared and would have trampled them had they not rolled into the stream. A shot echoed in the silence, and Bird Hunter feared for his women. He knocked the intruder unconscious with a rock and turned to find Fawna and her mother standing over the dead body of the third man. Yahanna straightened, in her hand a fresh scalp. Lifting it above her head, she smiled and sank to the ground.

There were many people from the village around them, called by the sound of the shot. Ready for a fight, the young warriors rode out to see if there were more men with the gang of trouble-makers.

Fawna knelt beside her mother and inspected the wound.

Slayer of Enemies dragged from the water the unconscious victim of Bird Hunter's rock. 'He is alive.'

Bird Hunter knelt beside his wife and her mother. 'He will be my gift to the women. He is the one who shot Yahanna.' Then he lifted Yahanna and carried her back to the village.

Fawna applied an ointment made of animal fat and herbs to the open wound on the woman's side. Then she packed mud over the salve. All the while her mother was watching her. 'You do well, daughter. That is as I would have done.'

'You are the one who taught me these things. Why should it not be done right?' Placing under her mother's head a pillow made of buffalo skins, she rocked back on her heels and studied Yahanna. 'How do you feel?'

'Very good. I have never felt better. It shames me that I fainted. Were there many to see?'

'There were many but they will sing of the woman who is brave, of the one who scalps those who would harm her.' A shudder ran through the girl as she thought of taking a scalp.

Patting her daughter's arm, Yahanna smiled. 'It is the way of our people. No one has said that only men can boast of their victories by showing their trophies.'

'Even now my husband is erecting a scalp pole for you so all will know you came to the aid of Bird Hunter.' She patted her mother's hand. 'But you should rest.'

'Rest? We have a captive. I want to join the women when he is stretched. I want to see him die. I want to be the last person he sees before he gives up his spirit.'

With great effort, she rose on one elbow to see Bird Hunter return with the scalp pole with its trophy glorifying the lodge of Yahanna.

Even though she was Kiowa, all of the people had learned to love Yahanna as a Comanche.

They brought pillows and robes for her to sit on beside the small fire which burned at the feet of the white man staked spreadeagle to the ground. With little dancing steps, the women circled his prone body. In their hands they held sharp sticks, dried turkey talons, and hickory switches to tear the skin and cause pain but not kill.

Yahanna's jaws were set with satisfaction as the man squirmed to escape the blows. His face was striped with red welts and scratches. An old woman leaned over him with a knife, bringing it closer and closer to his neck until he let out a weak cry of fear. The women laughed to see his fright. Their men were taught not to show such weakness or fear. Beyond the circle of the fire, the braves watched silently as the women took their just revenge.

The old woman slipped the knife into the collar of his shirt and ripped it open, uncovering a chest of thick black hair. Tracing a small circle on the man's skin with the point of her knife, she swiftly lifted a swatch of hair, leaving underneath a raw wound oozing blood.

Holding the swatch of hair above her head, the old woman called Yahanna. 'I have scalped his chest, Yahanna! Can I put this on a pole before my lodge?'

'The people will think you are Osage with scalps of coyotes and dogs over the lodges,' Yahanna laughed.

The wife of Man Who Shivers in the Sun stepped forward and slowly drew the dried talons of a hawk across the bleeding chest. He screamed only once and fainted.

'He does not like to play in our games,' said the wife of Man Who Shivers in the Sun in a high-pitched voice. Slowly she poured cold water from a clay jug over the unconscious white man. His eyelids fluttered and opened, and she danced to her place in the circle.

Slowly, painfully Yahanna rose. Everyone waited to see what the beloved Kiowa would do. Favoring her wound, she leaned over him and removed the cowhide belt from around his waist. Weakly at first, gathering strength, she whipped him across the stomach and chest. Each lash of the broad leather made bleeding lesions. When he fainted for the second time, she stopped and returned to her seat of honor.

Into the night the women kept their captive awake until the pain no longer seemed to affect him.

Falcon Man stepped into the circle of women. 'He will die if you continue. Why not allow him to rest until the sun is new, and he will be more aware of his punishment.'

Before they left, the old woman checked his bindings to make sure he could not escape during the night.

Neither Fawna nor Dataha had taken part in the women's revenge and were relieved when their chief ended it for the night.

'Do you think the other women will say we have hearts of rabbits?' Fawna asked.

'The mother of your husband didn't take part. None of the wives of Falcon Man took part. We will not worry about what some of the others might think.'

In the morning Yahanna leaned over her prize with the shining blade reflecting red rays of sunshine. He seemed to know that the time for dying had arrived. His eyes were tightly closed; he whimpered the sound of a frightened puppy as she traced a line around the top of his head with the keen point. Quickly the hair lock was lifted and he gasped and died.

Holding the scalp above her head, Yahanna walked among the women, displaying her trophy. A second badge was added to her scalp pole.

Vindicated, the village gradually returned to normal.

CHAPTER TWENTY

Eagle Hunting rode at the head of the small band among the ruins of their village. The soldiers had used their wagon gun first. Lodges had been blown apart and the possessions of his people broken and destroyed. What ever remained was set afire. Anger raced through him with the burning of a thousand camp fires.

He dismounted where his own lodge had been. A doll his wife had made for their daughter was charred and broken. In his mind he pictured his daughter holding her treasured doll. He lost control.

He rallied his men and inflamed them with

bitter words. 'This would have been another of their wars on women and children. Comanches can do the same, only better. We will ride and we will kill. What would it have been if Bird Hunter had not had his vision?' Angrily he challenged them. 'Tall Man, where your lodge stood would also have been the body of your good woman with the baby she carries torn from her body and shot in the dust by the wagon gun. Are we men that will allow this?'

Only Little Warrior remained silent.

'If this is what the white men call war, then we will give them their war!' Eagle Hunting shouted, the veins standing out along his temple. 'We will ride. There is a family of whites who live in the mud houses very close. There we will start.'

Less than a half day's ride away was the sod house of a farmer. His one room house was dug into the side of a hill. In that house lived the farmer, his wife, and three children, the family Eagle Hunting singled out in his anger.

Leaping to the back of his horse, he and his angry followers galloped toward the sod house and its unsuspecting occupants.

Little Warrior followed reluctantly in the rear. As a novice, he had no voice in the affairs of men. It would be these men who would decide when he was a man and could sit among them. He wondered if Bird Hunter would approve of this raid.

When the sun passed the middle of the sky, they could see the farmer's clay house. They kept a grove of trees to their backs, and the farmer could not see them as he followed the mule pulling his plow. The farmer removed his hat, ran his fingers through his hair, and wiped his brow with his sleeve. A girl of about six brought a pail of water to him. He drank two dippers full, then poured the remaining water over his head. At that moment he looked toward the Indians but did not see them. He hesitated. Replacing his hat, he sent the girl back to the house. He turned again to his plow.

Eagle Hunting kicked his mount and swept toward the farmer. A woman screamed from the house. It was too late. He was frantically pulling the revolver from the waist band of his pants when he died on Eagle Hunting's spear.

Tall Man swung from the back of his horse and grabbed the girl. Her water pail flew from her hand, and the dry ground sucked hungrily at the few drops of water that was left.

At first it seemed the woman ran toward them. Then she lifted a long-barreled rifle and fired. Fast Runner toppled backwards over the rump of his horse, a bullet hole in his chest. From the doorway a second rifle blast came and Little Warrior's horse sagged to the ground. A boy not much younger than himself had fired the shot. Little Warrior rolled in the dirt. Eagle Hunting held the woman down with her own weapon as she kicked furiously. With one fatal blow of his knife, Eagle Hunting stilled her. Two braves rushed the house as another rifle blast sounded. Then all was quiet. One brave staggered to the door, his hand pressed tightly to his stomach. Blood gushed between his fingers. After a few shaky steps in the yard, he stumbled. He was dead before he hit the ground.

Tall Man had the little girl under his arm. She did not cry but scratched and clawed until he set her down. As soon as her feet touched the ground, she ran to her mother.

Her mother, her father, her brother . . . all three were dead. Only she and a baby too small to walk were left.

With the memory of his daugher's doll in his mind, Eagle Hunting held his hand over the squalling baby's mouth until he dropped it and the body lay lifeless at his feet. Crazed with anger, Eagle Hunting took the scalps of the farmer and his wife. He also took the revolver and the six-year-old daughter.

Mounted on the horse of Running Man, Little Warrior rode slowly, almost certain he would be sick. If Bird Hunter had been their leader, this would not have happened. Little Warrior wrestled with the shame.

Nearing the village, they heard the wail of the white man's army horn. The sound was not good. It was not as the soldiers would play it.

When they entered the village, the cold eyes of Falcon Man were upon them. Little Warrior could feel his disapproval.

The small band waited in strained silence as Eagle Hunting stood before the chief. 'What is the meaning of this?' The chief pointed out the white girl who stood paralyzed with fright.

When he finished his story, Eagle Hunting waited.

'You did not go from this place to make war,' said Falcon Man. 'Your duty was to see if it was safe for our women to go after our lodges. After this, our women will not be safe here in our village. Dogs that follow the scraps from our cooking fires will not be safe. You have disgraced our name. Two good men have died following you. From this day on, you are not a Kwahadies Comanche. You will not speak to any member of our tribe. That includes your wife and your children. Take what you have with you and leave. Killer of Women will be your name. When you meet a Comanche, he will not speak but he will spit on you. This is my command.'

Falcon Man spat on Killer of Women, once called Eagle Hunting, and turned his back on him.

For the rest of the day and all night, the chiefs sat at the council fire. Each of them was heard. Slayer of Enemies walked slowly around the fire and stopped in front of Bird Hunter. Then he spoke softly but forcefully.

'I, Slayer of Enemies, am a Comanche. I am a husband. I am a father. Soon I hope to be a grandfather. But first I am Comanche. As a husband and a father I might have done shameful things but never as a Comanche.' He continued his walk silently and stopped in front of Falcon Man.

'My son's medicine is a white man. I ask that my son be allowed to take the white girl to this white man and request a meeting with the Chief of the Soldiers. Let him explain what has happened and why. Let him tell them that the one who did this thing, Killer of Women, has been banned from the tribe and now wanders the land without a family or home or friends. This is my wish.'

Man Who Shivers in the Sun rose and drew his robe close about him to help ward off the chill of early morning air. He too was a proud Comanche. His voice, unlike that of Slayer of Enemies, shook with age and illness. In silence he waited, pulling his robe more tightly about him.

'I too have a son, Little Warrior. He will soon be a man, walking among the tallest of men with pride. If I could change places with Slayer of Enemies and my son could change places with his son, my words might differ from Slayer of Enemies' words. For us to send a son to the white soldiers' camp now would surely condemn him to die. It is their way. They have ears, but they do not hear. Perhaps their ears are to keep the big hats from covering their eyes. We can talk, but it will have no meaning. They do not understand our hearts or our ways because they have no desire to. It will mean nothing to them that we have banned Killer of Women from us.'

He stalked the warmth of the fire and stopped in front of Bird Hunter. 'I see before me the youngest of our war chiefs. I am proud of him and can imagine how his father feels. My pride would surely burst from me in tears of joy if my son someday becomes such a Comanche. I ask that everything be considered before we ask our young chief to go to the camp of the white soldiers.'

Each member of the council spoke. By then the sun was in the middle of the morning sky. No one had risen from the council fire, which was their way. Being the youngest, Bird Hunter could speak only after all others had spoken, when it was his turn to speak, the council was drawing to a close.

He had never spoken before the council. He wanted to say the right words and was nervous. The palms of his hands were wet.

'I am proud of Shivering Man. I am proud

of my father. I am proud of my mother and my wife. But most of all, I am proud that I am a Comanche. I would be honored to do this thing my father suggested. I will take the white girl to her people. Once before I returned a white girl to them. My own father has known the friendship of these people. There is no danger.'

Bird Hunter leaned forward in his earnestness. 'Swede will stand by me when I talk with The Leader of the Soldiers.'

'We do not fear the one called Swede so much,' Falcon Man said, 'but he may not be able to save you from the army.'

'But what has been done must be faced. If we make no attempt, they will think we are all guilty of Killer of Women's cowardly act.'

Falcon Man placed his hand on the shoulder of the young man. 'Your words are as pure as the mountain stream. It is truly my hope that Swede is your medicine, for you will need something strong when you confront the soldier chief. They do not accept us as people; therefore they will not accept you as a man of our people.'

'We must try.' Bird Hunter knew again the nervousness in his stomach which always came over him when Falcon Man spoke to him.

* * *

Fawna longed to ask Bird Hunter not to go. She feared for him. But instead of asking him to stay, she helped him prepare for the trip, packing food and an extra doe skin shirt she had made for him. She had to stand on her toes to reach the back of big grey stallion.

'Come around here, woman,' he commanded when she had finished. Climbing over a log, she stood waiting in front of him. Sitting on the log, he pulled her to his lap and held her tightly. Her face flushed red with pleasure and embarrassment when some of the other women saw them and laughed softly together.

'They are watching.'

'Let them watch. They only envy you that you have a husband who cares for you even when you are not in bed.'

'You are without shame,' she said but there was no scorn in her voice.

'Why else would I have married a Kiowa when there are so many pretty Comanche women?'

She hit him on the shoulder with the palm of her hand. 'They would not have you. Women prefer a man who does not always place himself in danger. Had I known you better, perhaps I would have passed you by also.'

His face sobered. 'Do I cause you pain because I want to do my best as a warrior of my people?'

'Sometimes.' Her voice was a weak whisper. And any other words between them would have to wait.

Little Warrior fidgeted anxiously a short distance away.

'Yes, Little Warrior?'

'You will need someone at your back,' he began timidly. 'I would like to be there when you go to the white soldiers.'

'You are still a novice. Are you ready for such an assignment?'

'The important thing is that you feel I am ready.'

Bird Hunter studied the boy for a moment. 'When one protects the back of another, he should do so with a heart so strong the other has no concern for what is behind him.'

'Perhaps you don't remember how difficult it is being a novice. One is neither a man nor a boy. There is no place for him. There is no fire to call his own. There is no woman to care for him.' The lad blushed, looking away from Fawna, but he went on with a strong heart. 'I have the best reason for making this request.' Bird Hunter could not help but notice the set of his jaw. 'No one would protect your back as I would,' Little Warrior ended.

'I will be proud to have you at my back. Go now and bid your family goodbye. We will leave soon.'

Walking away, there was a boyish spring to Little Warrior's step, yet the carriage of a man.

Bird Hunter faced Fawna and waited for her to speak. When she did not, he voiced what he thought was in her heart.

'I know he is young but there was a time when I was in his place. I *do* remember. It has been a very short while ago. The grass has turned green only seven times since Kato and I raided the horses of the Osage. I remember well what Little Warrior suffers.'

'I would feel better if someone older, more experienced were at your back. Can't you understand that?'

'He is small and he is young, but his heart is that of a man many times older and larger than he. If something should happen to my back, it would be only after he is dead. I know this, I have no fear. You must trust my judgment. Had he not asked me, I would have asked for him.'

'Truly?'

'Truly.'

Bird Hunter looked back as he rode away. His mother, Fawna and Dataha stood apart from the men in silence. His heart went out to Dataha. She was thinking of the day Kato did not return from the fort. Ahead of him rode Little Warrior, leading a mare gentle enough for the child to ride. The youngster held the horse's mane with both hands, her eyes on Little Warrior's back. She seemed to trust the young brave.

To the north, lodge poles were being cut. The Comanches stopped work to watch them go. There was an ominous silence and Bird Hunter resisted the urge to wave. Kneeing the stallion, he rode ahead of Little Warrior to set a pace easy for the child to follow.

CHAPTER TWENTY-ONE

Lars greeted him warmly at the Swensen ranch. 'Well, what have we here? Another daughter for me?'

'No, friend. I have instead a request.'

'First you must come in the house and see my son. Have some coffee and tell me what I can do for you.'

Little Warrior lifted the girl down from her horse and both of them stood back shyly, waiting.

'Bird Hunter!' Alfa called. 'We have not seen you for so long. Who are your friends? Where is No Toe Foot?'

'No Toe Foot is dead.'

'Dead! How could that be?' Swede's sympathy touched Bird Hunter.

Bird Hunter told him of No Toe Foot's shameful death.

'I heard about that, not knowing it was No Toe Foot. I was ashamed of my people. There was no reason for it.'

'No Toe Foot was a warrior and should have died as one.'

The Swede shook his head sadly. 'Now come in the house. All of you.'

'This is Little Warrior. He is small but very brave. I am lucky to have such a brave warrior riding at my back.'

'It is always lucky to have a brave man behind you. Come in the house, Little Warrior and have coffee with us.' In English he spoke to his wife. 'Have we food for our friends, my dear?'

'I can fry some eggs.'

'Good.' Turning back to the child, he asked, 'What is your name?'

'Debra.'

When he extended his hand to her, Debra took it and followed him into the house.

Shanda stood apart from all of them, against the wall. *How she has changed*! Bird Hunter thought. She was no longer the little girl he had brought to the Swensen ranch. She was a young woman. 'Ask her to come forward so I can talk to her.'

'Shanda, come here. Bird Hunter wants to speak to you.'

Slowly the girl came forward and stood with lowered eyes.

'Ask her if she is happy.'

Her nod was answer enough.

'Our son is like her own child. She takes care of him continually and some day she will be a fine mother.'

'She has become a very beautiful young woman and soon all the young men will be fighting for her hand,' said Bird Hunter.

She blushed. Obviously the Swede had been teaching her some Comanche.

'Owen Wilkes, the young soldier you sent to us has already called. He is very much taken with her.'

Alfa brought the baby to show him off. Lifting the boy above his head, Bird Hunter smiled up at him, and the baby drooled in his face.

'He is teething, Bird Hunter.'

'It is the way with babies, Indian and white. Someday I hope to have a son of my own and a girl. Maybe three or four of each. My wife is not yet with child.'

He did not notice Shanda's reaction but Alfa placed her arm around the girl's shoulder and led her to the kitchen.

'Come, let's prepare eggs and coffee while the men talk.'

In the kitchen, Alfa studied the girl she had grown to love. 'It was a shock to you to learn that Bird Hunter is married. Why is that, Shanda? Have you been thinking of him in what we women might call a romantic way?'

'I guess so.' Shanda would not look at Alfa.

'He's an Indian, child.'

There was a hint of hostility in her eyes. 'He was an Indian when he brought me here to you unharmed. There are many white men who would not have done that. He is a good person and I like him.'

'Yes, I like him, too. We all like him. I cannot count all the times Lars and I have talked about him in the last year. We enjoy having him here, and I think he enjoys our company too. However, I think he would be more comfortable if we would build a fire in the yard and sit around it on the ground. He is very uncomfortable in the house.'

Shanda smiled. 'I have seen him look at the ceiling three or four times just since he arrived.'

Alfa pulled the coffee pot to the edge of the stove. 'You pour the coffee, and I'll take the eggs in.'

Little Warrior and Bird Hunter looked at the eggs hesitantly.

'Is there something wrong?' Swede asked.

'What are these?'

'Eggs.'

'We drink them from shells. Uncooked.'

'Try them this way. I think you'll like them,' Lars suggested.

Bird Hunter took a bite while Little Warrior waited for his reaction. As a smile spread over his leader's face, Little Warrior cautiously took a bite and was pleased. At the foot of the table, Debra ate ravenously.

'What is your last name, Debra?'

'Braydon. But Indians killed mama, and

daddy and my big brother and my baby brother.'

The Swede told Bird Hunter what the child had said to him.

Bird Hunter nodded and told him how Killer of Women had disgraced the Comanche people.

'It was the act of a sick man, and he has been banned from our tribe.'

When Lars translated for his wife Bird Hunter's reason for coming to them, and his story about Killer of Women, she was visibly disturbed.

'I don't think it is a good idea for Bird Hunter to go. The army has been as much at fault as the Comanche for the troubles we've had. They might not understand his gesture as it is intended.'

'He feels if there is going to be any peace, it must begin somewhere. The return of the child is their way.'

Alfa was not able to dissuade them and her despair was obvious. The three men and the child, Debra Braydon, left the ranch for the fort. Lars drove a buggy so the child could rest and sleep. As they passed through the low, rolling hills, Bird Hunter and Little Warrior kept a constant vigil for their safety. Less than two hours from the fort, they sighted a detail of soldiers.

'There are soldiers beyond the hill,' Bird Hunter said.

'Perhaps both of you'd better stay close to the buggy so they will know you are with me.'

'That may do no good, but we'll try it.' Bird Hunter signaled for Little Warrior to return. They rode in silence behind their white friend, every nerve electrified. Beyond a small copse, they emerged into the open and advanced slowly toward the soldiers. Bird Hunter saw first one of the Indian scouts who rode with the army. In a secluded area behind a dead tree, the scout watched their advance.

'One of the fort Indians is watching!'

'Then he will see there is no danger to me, that we travel together.'

Soon the Indian disappeared, and soldiers reappeared on the hill, resting their mounts, waiting in silence with drawn rifles, forming a line across the path of the trio. Lars drew back on the lines and stopped the vehicle. Debra raised up and looked at the soldiers.

'Why are they there?' she asked.

'They are waiting for us, Debra.' Lars reached out and drew the girl close to him. 'Are you all right?'

'Yes, sir.'

'Good. Don't you worry about a thing.' A young lieutenant accompanied by the Indian scout rode forward to meet them. 'Good afternoon, Lieutenant.'

'Good afternoon. Mr. Swensen, isn't it?'

'Yes.'

'What is the meaning of this, Mr.

Swensen? Why are you with these Comanches?'

Briefly Lars explained the reason for their visit.

'Take their weapons.' The lieutenant spoke to the Indian scout.

'Why?' Lars rose from the buggy seat. 'They come in peace. For what reason do you take their weapons?'

'They are Comanches.'

'They are peaceful!' When Swede questioned the lieutenant's order, the scout paused and waited for a decision between the two white men. Bird Hunter could feel the tension between them. He too waited.

'If I take them into the fort with weapons, the colonel will give me all kinds of hell, Mr. Swensen.'

'You are not taking them to the fort. I am. In fact, you could say they are coming in on their own. This whole thing is their idea.'

After a long hesitation, he said to the Indian, 'Let them keep their weapons.' To Lars he said, 'I will ride beside you, Mr. Swensen.'

When the Indian scout dropped behind them, Little Warrior remained a few feet behind the strange Indian. It became a silent contest between them to see who would ride behind the other.

'Lieutenant, why don't you instruct your man to come up here beside the buggy. He is not going to be able to ride behind my friends.'

The officer motioned for the scout to come up beside him. The officer called ahead to the sergeant of the detail to ride ahead. 'I will stay here with Mr. Swensen.'

The sergeant barked orders to his men and rode ahead.

'It is very strange, Mr. Swensen. How can you explain it?'

'It is up to Bird Hunter to explain it to your commanding officer, Lieutenant . . . What is your name?'

'Collier, sir. Anthony Collier.'

'Been at the fort long?'

'Less than a month.'

'Right out of West Point?'

'Almost.' Turning in the saddle, he looked back at Bird Hunter and Little Warrior. 'They are very young. Who are they?'

'The taller one is Bird Hunter. He is a war chief. The other is Little Warrior. He is what they consider a novice.'

'What does that mean?'

'He has not yet proven himself in battle. He is neither a boy nor a man. With acts of bravery, like coming here with Bird Hunter, he will prove himself and be accepted.'

'How old are they?'

'Bird Hunter is twenty or twenty-one and Little Warrior about fourteen.'

'They are both young.'

'No, Lieutenant. The Comanche is never young. And he is never too old. From birth, the Comanche boys are sons of the whole tribe, cared for by every adult. They are not expected to do menial chores as the girls are. They get the choicest meat and more food than girls. As soon as they can walk, they can ride. Not like you and I ride but as warriors. Boys are considered the only means of survival for their people. They are trained to defend their tribe from all invaders, to the death.

'Right now, Mr. Collier, you and I are invaders. We are here uninvited on land that has been theirs longer than our history. If they decided this land is not enough for them and moved east into Ohio or Illinois, we would react, with justification, as they have.'

Lars was pleased with the way Collier was listening and accepting what he said, so he went on.

'Nothing is going to change them. Not in our life-time! They fear nothing, man or beast. Even with our highly-developed weaponry, one of them will equal five or more of us. They do not question a command. If Bird Hunter told that boy to attack you and your men now, he would do so without a second thought because he has been trained for that since he was born. Can you say the same for the men following you, Mr. Collier?'

'No, sir, I cannot.'

‘I said they are never too old. They will fight until death. They are not a pleasant enemy. And they have never heard of Napolean or studied his tactics, but they could have taught him some tricks. With men like them, Napoleon could have changed the story of Waterloo.’

‘You sure think highly of them.’

‘A better friend a man cannot have. They have earned my respect.’

‘It is strange for a white man to feel as you do.’

‘Why is it strange? They can live on land that you and I would starve on. When we came here, we brought supplies from the east so we could make it from one season to the next. That’s an advantage they don’t have, yet look at them. You would be invincible with a command of men like them.’

‘What is Bird Hunter like?’

‘That is the third white child he has saved.’ Lars told him about Shanda and the soldier named Wilkes.

‘I know Wilkes. I’ve never heard about being saved by Bird Hunter.’

‘Good things have a way of getting lost among the bad, do they not?’

‘Unfortunately.’ Lieutenant Collier looked back at Bird Hunter. ‘It was truly strange that he let Trooper Wilkes go free in view of what was happening.’

‘What is strange about a good man putting

out a hand to one less fortunate, Lieutenant?'
'At that point, Mr. Swensen, I'm afraid I lapse into the theory that they are savages.'

CHAPTER TWENTY-TWO

A heavy gate was now installed across the opening where No Toe Foot's raiding party had entered the new fort. Lars could hear the guard call to alert the Command, as the gate swung open. They were met by a short, fat man wearing a colonel's eagle on his shoulders.

'Lieutenant,' he snapped, 'why did you let these savages enter with their weapons?'

'That was my doing, Colonel,' said Swensen. 'I suggested that the lieutenant not disarm them. They come in peace.'

'Who the hell are you? My officers take orders from me, not you! Lieutenant Collier! Disarm them *now*!'

Swensen spoke in Comanche to Bird Hunter. 'The colonel would like the surrender of your weapons. It would be a show of good faith.'

'Do you think I should?'

'I don't know. Maybe it would be best.' He turned back to face the colonel, anger in his face, 'Sir, these men are here to return this child. They did not need to come here but hoped you were a fair man.'

'How did they get a white child?'

Swensen told the colonel the story of the banishment of Killer of Women. He explained that Bird Hunter had come to him for help in returning the girl.

'I've heard about Indian lovers,' snarled the colonel. 'They will be treated as they deserve, like savages.' Turning to a burly sergeant, he barked, 'Lock them in the guardhouse.'

'Just a damn minute, Colonel.' Lars jumped out of the buggy angrily. 'Would you do the same with the commanding officer of another army? Bird Hunter is a war chief of the Comanches, and he came here in good faith.'

'If this Indian lover says one more word, lock him up too, Sergeant.'

The sergeant pulled Little Warrior roughly from his horse, and Bird Hunter charged. Little Warrior came up with the sergeant's revolver and was about to shoot the colonel when the soldier nearby jumped him and knocked him to the ground. Bird Hunter wheeled and drew back on the reins, making his horse rear and land with its front feet on the soldier's back.

Using a rifle as a club, a soldier knocked Bird Hunter from his horse into the dust, where the young chief lay unconscious.

Two more soldiers held Lars on both sides. With little effort the big Swede shook himself free and shook his fist at the fat commanding officer. 'Washington is going to hear of this, Colonel!' Four soldiers grabbed the Swede and dragged him out of range of the colonel.

'See what you caused, Lieutenant,' yelled the colonel.

'Lieutenant Collier did not cause this,' argued Swensen. 'You are the son of a bitch who caused this, Colonel. The President will hear of this if I have to storm his office in Washington.'

'You'll go no place, Indian lover.' His voice broke with anger, his fat face red, the veins in his neck standing out like rope. 'Lock him up in the guardhouse with his friends. And if any harm has been done to this child, there might be a hanging. Corporal, take the girl to the surgeon.'

Angrily, Lars Swensen strained to escape. Little Warrior also struggled but he could not free himself from the many hands holding him. He could not get to his chief, who lay with blood-stained face in the dirt.

A young Choctaw called Small Man Leaning watched the action unnoticed. For almost a year he had scouted for the white soldiers, but until now he had never seen anything which made him proud to be Indian. His people were suppressed. No longer were there warriors to fight but old women shifted from one deadly place to another living from garbage of the white men.

They would die in ever-ravaged camps, confined by the whites, and seem thankful for the privilege. He shifted his weight from the shorter right leg to the left leg. What he had just seen was red men, fighting back! Quietly he slipped out through the heavy gate.

Once outside, he tore off the army hat band and insignia and clapped the hat back on his head. Because he was crippled, it was usually difficult for him to mount the big bay furnished to him by the army, but today he mounted with surprising ease. Sitting tall in his saddle, he squared his shoulders, kicking the horse's flanks. He hoped he had the tracking skills of his forefathers; he must find the brave young warrior's people.

At sundown he saw a ranch that could belong to the Comanche's white friend, but he did not stop. He rode into the night, toward the Indian village destroyed by the wagon gun and torch. From there, if his father's blood was still in his veins, he could find the trail of the tribe.

Small Man Leaning felt shame at the sight of the destroyed Comanche village where people had once lived, laughing and crying together, sharing happy and sad times. The cannon had left nothing unscathed. He nudged the big bay with his heel and slowly circled the remains of the village until he saw parallel marks where travois had trailed along the ground. He saw foot prints of the people, some tiny ones of children which burned in his mind. Had they been here, they would have been killed by the soldiers.

In a steady canter, Small Man Leaning followed the marks along the ground. They led northward with no signs of stopping. No cooking fires were made along the route. They had moved very hurriedly, and he had to find them . . . soon.

Even now Bird Hunter might be dead.

CHAPTER TWENTY-THREE

Little Warrior brushed the dirt from Bird Hunter's wound. He tried to comfort his chief. Lars dipped a piece of cloth torn from his shirt into the bucket of water in the corner of the cell.

'Use this, Little Warrior.'

'I have failed my chief. I should be dead. My duty was to protect his back, and I did not.' He dabbed at the wound and squeezed water from the rag into the torn flesh. 'There are many braves he could have chosen, but he took me because I am young and need to prove myself. He is wounded and captive because I was not man enough to protect him.'

'Bird Hunter will not blame you. If it is anyone's fault, it is mine or that of the stupid colonel. Don't blame yourself. I could have brought Debra here myself, and none of this would have happened!'

Lars walked to the door and looked out through the tiny opening. He could see only one side of the gate and the guard post on top. If the gate were open, he would be able to see the town to the east on top of the next hill. He hoped the townspeople would soon learn of his plight and get him out. Then he would be in a position to help Bird Hunter.

* * *

Small Man Leaning surveyed the Comanche camp. He hesitated. They might kill him before he could explain. He could not blame them. He had helped the white man many times against them. If they killed him, it was what he deserved. He must do it for Bird Hunter and for his new feeling of self respect. *Let them do what they will*, he thought, braced for the first meeting.

Comanches surrounded him on all sides. They appeared like disturbed hornets out of the ground. A tall aging man who resembled the young chief at the fort, confronted him.

'Who are you and why are you here?'

Small Man Leaning knew only a little of the Comanche language but he understood the question.

'I am Small Man Leaning. Choctaw.'

'What kind of man are you who rides a beautiful horse until he is near death?'

'I bring urgent word to the chief of Bird Hunter.'

'I am Slayer of Enemies. Bird Hunter is my son. What have you, a Choctaw, to say about my son?'

When Small Man Leaning explained why he was there, the chief studied him closely.

'Falcon Man will decide what to do.' He motioned to a young novice. 'Give the Choctaw your horse and lead him to the village. His will surely die if it must carry any one a step farther.'

The Choctaw unbuckled the pistol belt at his waist and handed the gun to Slayer of Enemies.

'This is not necessary, new friend,' Slayer of Enemies protested.

'I would feel better. If I am among you unarmed, I show more trust in you. It is the way of my people. Most of them carry no weapons.'

'No weapons?'

'We have long been the victims of defeat. Our villages are only where the white men will allow them.'

'Are you a tribe of women?'

'With a heavy heart, I must answer, yes. This is my chance to prove that I would not be like them. I wish to be more like the Comanche who is feared by the white men. In the faces of the white men I could see fear when your son and the younger Comanche came into the fort. Not fear of a whole tribe, but of one warrior and a brave boy. It made my heart happy to see that fear.'

In the circle of tipis, Falcon Man waited.

Slayer of Enemies spoke hurriedly. 'Small Man Leaning has sought our village for three suns to help save Bird Hunter and Little Warrior.'

'A good and brave man, this Choctaw. Sit down and we will talk.'

When Small Man Leaning described Bird Hunter's capture, Falcon Man rose and walked apart from the others. Soon he returned and pointed at Dataha's brother Nacato. 'Go to our friends, the Kiowas. Little Mountain is closest. He may see fit to send word to Satanta. Tell them we need their help. We are going to ride against the fort of the white soldiers.'

Swiftly, silently Nacato left for the Kiowa camp. Behind him he led a second horse so he could ride without stopping to rest his animal.

There was anger in the voice of Falcon Man. 'It is my place to lead. Shivering Man will stay here and protect our women and children. Slayer of Enemies will be my right hand and will protect my back.'

Small Man Leaning watched the Comanches organize their war with as much ease as they would a game. He began to feel a new hope, a new pride he had never known before.

'I would like to ride with you.'

Falcon Man paused. 'Some of your people are with the white soldiers even as we talk. Would you make war against them?'

'This is my time to become a man. For too long I have ridden the woman's trail. If I can become one of you, I can change.'

'Then it is agreed.'

'I know the fort. Your men would have a better chance. Beyond the large gate is a small one not seen from the trail. It will break easily if we need to use it.'

'Take a horse from my herd and go with the first band. There will be a second band to follow after we leave. It is the Comanche way. If the first band is seen, no one will know how many we number.' A brief smile played over the chief's face. 'Many times we have surprised the enemy with our true numbers. There will be even more surprises this time for the soldiers.'

Small Man Leaning was truly surprised when they rode out. Almost two hundred braves rode from the valley at the headwaters of the Red River. Some came from a camp among the foothills, and still to come were the Kiowas. Falcon Man had called on his friends. Seventy of Little Mountain's Kiowa warriors and two hundred Comanches led by

Peta Nocona from the Nocona band would come.

'Falcon Man. Slayer of Enemies. I greet you,' Peta said as he rode abreast of his friends. 'There are many brave men at your back, Falcon Man. We will show the white soldiers what it means to stir the anger of the Comanches and their friends. There will be much dying when we arrive . . . and this is a good time to die!' He chanted the old Indian saying taught him by his grandfather and his grandfather before him. They all knew to die righting a wrong was a good time to die.

'Peta, how is your wife and your young son Quanah?'

'The Spirits smile on them. By the time we have destroyed the fort, Cynthia Ann will have borne me another son. Even as we talk he may be kicking his way into this world of men.' Peta patted his horse's neck. 'Have no fear for your son, Slayer of Enemies. We will free him from this trap he has sprung on himself. Once he has returned safely to his robes and his wife, he will not trust the whites again. It will make him a stronger Comanche.'

Peta looked behind him. Clouds of dust arose from the hundreds of horses. 'Look, my friends! Our dust will settle beyond the western mountains in the pots of the Utes! They too will know the Comanche rides.'

Each man had brought with him a spare

horse. A thousand unshod hooves beat the dry earth, sending up billows of dust. The billows rolled together in a solid mass that shadowed the sun.

A smile crept over Peta's dark face.

'Why do you smile?' asked Slayer of Enemies.

'In my inner eye, I saw myself dead at the very moment my son will be born. Inside my head I could hear the songs my people will sing about me and about the new Peta. For surely my soul will enter the body of my newest son. The white world would cringe when they discover the Nocona Comanche lives forever.'

Slayer of Enemies smiled. 'This is a very big thought. A very grand idea indeed. But it will not be.'

'Why not?'

'You will not die in this battle. You will live forever. The sons of your son's sons will hang around your knee and listen to stories of this battle that will fall from your toothless mouth. May the spirits give them enough wisdom to know the truth from the lies. For you will not remember everything as it really happened.'

'You are a wise man. May your son also give you many grandsons to hang on your knees and listen to your lies.'

They laughed together. Very wise, Peta could see that the mirth of his friend came only from his teeth. In his heart he feared for Bird Hunter. A wise man knows when to leave a man with his fears, and Peta returned to the two hundred braves who followed him.

That day it was difficult to tell when the sun truly set. For most of the day it had been hidden from view behind the dust.

CHAPTER TWENTY-FOUR

In the guardhouse, Bird Hunter raised up on his elbow and rubbed the back of his head.

'How do you feel?' Lars asked.

'There is a herd of wild horses in my head, my mouth is as dry as the belly of a lizard, and my eyes hurt. Where are we?'

'In the soldiers' guardhouse. Under arrest,' Swensen answered, giving him a cup of water.

Little Warrior broke his hour-long vigil at the window to sit by his chief. 'My heart is very heavy to see you like this. If I had been more of a man, they would not have been able to hit you from behind.'

'You are man enough. We were like a tiny crumb of food dropped into an ant's nest. If I had not led you here, you would be sitting at our fires now.'

Swede said, 'When word reaches the town, many of my friends will object to such treatment. The colonel can't turn his back on the people without causing trouble for himself.' He looked carefully at the wound on Bird Hunter's head. 'I see why you have wild horses in your head. It will hurt for quite a while.'

Little Warrior whispered, 'See the soldier with long white hair and a wrinkled face who uses his knife to sharpen the stick? Most of the day he has sharpened the stick.'

Bird Hunter saw the old corporal sitting near the horse pens. His grey hair hung to his shoulders. His face was crisscrossed by thousands of wrinkles, his only apparent concern the long stick he whittled. Slowly, with each turn of the stick, a thin shaving rolled up before the blade of his knife and floated to the ground. Noises from the soldiers did not distract him. Bird Hunter was reminded of the old man who tended horses for his people. The corporal also seemed to be a tender of horses.

'What is it about this man that is of interest to you, Little Warrior?'

'When he finishes with the sticks he carves, he throws them aside. When he is finished each stick is as sharp as the knife he cuts with.' Little Warrior rubbed his hands together and smiled.

Bird Hunter read his thoughts. 'We will try to get one of them.'

Lars watched the front gate. 'I hoped I

would be able to talk to the colonel. Legally he cannot hold me and I thought he would realize that by now. If I were outside, I could help you. But in here, I'm helpless.'

'No man is helpless as long as he has breath, Swede.'

'You are right, Bird Hunter. I was thinking of Alfa, and the baby, and Shanda at the ranch alone. If I could get word to my friend, McLin, he could tell them what has happened.'

'We will tell her ourselves . . . while she fries white man's eggs for us as she did before.'

'What are you planning?' Lars sat on the floor near the door listening to Bird Hunter's plan.

'What you have in mind is wrong. With a weapon in your hand, even a sharp stick, you become a hostile enemy.'

'No Toe Foot was not hostile, he was already their captive, when they hanged him from the wall.'

'I heard that you hanged one of the soldiers and a scout. Is that true?'

'Yes, in the white way. As the whites have taught us. And then the white soldiers fired at us with their wagon gun afterwards. They would have killed their own men if we had not already done it for them.'

'I must remember to report that when we are out of here. My words to the colonel were not idle threats. I intend to make a full report to Washington. I hope the President reads my letter, not someone like the colonel.'

'What do you mean, write?'

'We put words on paper, and the stage coach takes the paper to the person we would write to.'

Bird Hunter sat quietly in the corner thinking about writing. He would like to be able to write to Fawna and tell her his feelings. He would tell her he had no desire for another wife. Fawna was enough wife for him.

* * *

As Bird Hunter was thinking of Fawna, she sought Dataha in the circle of tipis to tell her the good news.

'You are going to have a baby?'

'Yes. When Falcon Man returns from the fort with Bird Hunter, I will tell him he is going to be a father.'

'Do you fear that he may not return? Then he would never know of the baby.'

'He is with the white man who is his medicine. He will return.'

Dataha studied the confidence in Fawna's face. If Kato had found his medicine, perhaps he would be alive now.

* * *

Falcon Man held up his hand and five hundred braves halted. He studied the flat land. The air was still. It would be foolish to expose themselves needlessly in the land between the hills and the fort. When Slayer of Enemies, Little Mountain, and Peta Nocona were beside him, he spoke.

'We will stay here until the darkness covers our dust while we move into fighting position. Peta, you will bypass the fort and take a position beyond it. Show yourself when the sun is first bright. Little Mountain will attack from the side where the cold winds blow. Slayer of Enemies will make his stand between them and their village. Some of the white men from the village may choose to help them. Beware! You could be attacked from your back.'

They would have the fort surrounded when the sun came up. They would have fresh mounts, for the horses they now rode could rest until after the battle. It was a good plan.

'We need to make ourselves ready and rest for tomorrow.'

There was much laughter among the younger men. They were anxious for the sun of a new day to go into battle with such men as Little Mountain, Peta Nocona, Falcon Man and Slayer of Enemies. For many of them it was their first fight against the white men.

Falcon Man listened to them and smiled, remembering. It was so very long ago. So many battles, so many men dead. The taste of battle was like sweet water. It was not their way to feel fear or to think of the possible outcome. Those laughing loudest could be dead tomorrow. If they should die, he would cry for them as all of his people would cry.

He called to Leaf Falling. 'Take a score of men and let yourself be seen from the fort. Do nothing to provoke the whites. If they send soldiers against you, do not fight but lead them here. There will be that many less protected by the wagon gun and the walls tomorrow.'

Leaf Falling hurried to round up his men. Falcon Man was pleased to see that Leaf Falling did not take the loudest and most reckless with him.

'Remember, they do not know that we know Bird Hunter has been captured. You are to be a stray band, carefree and aimless, so they will not be forewarned.'

'I understand, Falcon Man.'

'Then go.'

The decoy band set out to lure some of the soldiers from the fort and were lost in the flashing sun of the open plains.

CHAPTER TWENTY-FIVE

Little Warrior watched the horse tender, as if willing the corporal to throw away the stick so Little Warrior could reach it. He heard men approaching and he leaped away from the window. The chain on the door rattled and the door swung open.

'Swensen, come with us!' ordered a sergeant blocking the open doorway.

'What about my friends?'

'I don't know nothin' about them. I'm supposed to take you to the colonel. Are you coming?'

'I'll get help,' Lars promised in Comanche.

Bird Hunter took hold of the big Swede's arm. 'When word of this reaches Falcon Man, even their wagon guns will not save them.'

'There are small ranchers and farmers who don't have wagon guns. Can nothing save them?'

Sadly Bird Hunter looked into his friend's eyes. They both knew the answer.

When Swensen was lost from sight, Little Warrior returned to the window where the old soldier carved his wood.

* * *

'Mr. Swensen, please have a seat.' The

colonel's tone was unduly friendly. Suddenly Lars saw Lawrence McLin waiting anxiously in an inner doorway.

Swensen took long strides across the room and shook his hand. 'Mac, can you help us?'

'I can help you, Amigo, but there is nothing I can do for the Indians. The colonel says he had you jailed in a fit of anger. He doesn't have a charge against you. You can go.'

'Hell, there is no charge against the Indians either.' Lars flared up again at the colonel. 'I have no intention of leaving here without my friends. They came here to do the right thing, and you, you overstuffed ass, treated them like criminals. What do you intend to do with them, Colonel?'

The colonel fumbled with ink bottles and quill on his desk. With great restraint, he looked up at the angry Swede and said with a biting edge to his words, 'This is a military matter of no concern to civilians. We will tend our own fires, Mr. Swensen.'

'You built a raging fire. You shot up and burned their village, which is why they attacked the homesteaders. Just where it all began is not so important. Where it ends is what counts. These men were trying to end the trouble when they returned the child to you. But you've shown how small you are by imprisoning them and making an example of them.'

'That's enough. Get out.'

'Like hell, it's enough. I said I won't leave without my friends. Turn them loose.'

The colonel sprang to his feet. His fat stomach heaved in and out with rapid breathing. His small eyes were sunken in the flabby face. 'Enough, I say! Leave while you can. Mr. Collier, see Mr. Swensen to the main gate.'

Lars started a new tirade. 'You better call four of the biggest men you have, Colonel.' With disgust Lars turned his back on him. 'It is difficult to deal with small men, Colonel, and you are really a small man. How did you get where you are? Do you have a brother-in-law who is a senator?'

Lieutenant Collier controlled himself with difficulty, for the colonel did have a brother-in-law in the Senate.

They were interrupted by a knock on the door. Anxious to divert the blond giant before him, the colonel called to the newcomer. 'Come in.'

'Major Daily reporting, sir.'

'What is it?'

Reluctant to speak, the major glanced at the civilians.

'Out with it, man.'

'Scouts report a band of Indians headed this way, sir.'

'How many?'

'About twenty.'

'Hell's fire, man! We can handle that many before breakfast.'

The colonel, feeling more secure, swaggered around the desk. 'Major, would you and Lieutenant Collier escort Mr. Swensen to the main gate?'

'I'll be d...'

'Swede,' Mac spoke softly. 'Come on, let's talk this over outside.'

To everyone's surprise Swensen followed McLin out of the room. When the door closed behind them, Mac said, 'You ain't gettin' nowhere with him. Let's go back to town and try to get a wire off to Washington and to General Cates at Fort Sill. If the gadget works, we'll have an answer before you make the colonel admit there is a problem. Also, it may be the only way you can keep your friends from being hung. That's just what's going to happen.'

'I know,' Swensen said weakly. 'I know.' His anger was spent.

CHAPTER TWENTY-SIX

What the scouts reported to Major Daily was a small band of well-chosen men who had been sent forward by Falcon Man to draw a detachment of troops from the fort. This small band camped less than an hour's ride from the main band. They laughed, they sang, they engaged in sports. Any trained scout could tell they were not an attack force. Falcon Man's plan for them to draw a detachment from the fort failed but the little band distracted the soldiers.

While the soldiers concentrated on this small band, they were less likely to discover the large force that would encircle them during the night.

'Do you want me to take a detail of men and roust them, sir?' asked Collier.

Major Daily studied for a moment. 'There's no way they could know yet what the colonel has done. They're probably a bunch of young hot heads spoiling for a skirmish. They'll tire of showing off soon. But double the guard, as a precaution, Lieutenant.'

'Yes, sir.' The young officer hurried to carry out his orders.

Major Daily lingered at the wall, uncertain of his interpretation of the Indian action.

Night closed like a door slamming . . . with sudden finality. Falcon Man passed orders to the five hundred Kiowa and Comanche braves to mount and split into four groups. Slowly, silently moved the army of skilled plains fighters.

Each chief passed Falcon Man in silence. First Peta Nocona, then Little Mountain, then Slayer of Enemies. Hidden partially by darkness, only the face of Slayer of Enemies showed concern, for it was his only son in the fort.

Falcon Man saw Small Man Leaning stop at a respectful distance. 'Do you have something to say, Choctaw?'

'Let me ride ahead and enter the fort. From inside I can open the small gate. With some luck, I might be able to destroy one or both of the wagon guns.'

'It is still a mystery why you should come to us. We are grateful that you told us about Bird Hunter and Little Warrior . . . but how can I be sure I can trust you, Small Man Leaning?'

'Send some of your men with me. Any of your men could kill me easily if what I say is not true. They are all better men than I. There is a way the cannons can be made useless!'

'How?'

'The fire hole can be plugged so the powder does not ignite.'

'You are sure? Have you ever done this?'

'I am sure of it, though I have never done it.'

'I will send men with you. If you get into the fort you will need help.'

'Are there two men who can stand without being seen?'

'There are two such men among us. Squirrel and Spotted Wolf, go with Small Man Leaning and follow his orders.'

‘Squirrel and I will gladly go, Falcon Man,’ said a small man with grey hair and a bright birthmark on his face.

The moon was high when the first scout rode back with a message Falcon Man had not wanted to hear.

‘They do not venture from the fort, Falcon Man, although they know our men are there.’

‘Our men should have made a poor attempt to hide. It is too late to think of that now. We will attack their fort as they did our village.’ He thought for a moment. ‘Did the Choctaw, Small Man Leaning, pass your point?’

‘I saw no one.’

‘Go back to your post. Tend your horses so they will be fresh if we need them.’

Before the sun had risen, Falcon Man’s men had reached their point of attack. They made almost no sound. For once, even the horses seemed to understand and were quiet as death. From his vantage point, the chief could see soldiers walk their posts along the top of the wall. He could also see the gaping mouth of the wagon gun on the wall facing him. His men would not be able to advance on the fort without facing the big gun. There was very little time.

* * *

Lars wired the President in Washington and the commanding general at Fort Sill. At dawn, there was still no answer from either. He paced the floor and for the hundredth time, stared anxiously out the front window of the telegraph office. His gaze took in the whole western sky. As the sun began to rise, he caught sight of movement. He strained to see better in the early light. Then he saw more clearly. Indians! There must be two hundred of them. He dashed out the door and came face-to-face with McLin.

'Have you see what is on the hill? To the west!'

'Oh, no . . . oh, no! If they come into town, there won't be any of us left. Look! To the north! Another hundred. We'd better get to the fort. The guards have not seen them or we would be hearing bugles. Take that horse tied at the rail in front of the telegraph office.' He ran for his own horse tied down the street in front of the restaurant.

Together they raced for the gate to the fort as the bugle sounded.

From the guardhouse, Bird Hunter tried to see beyond the large gate. Behind him, Little Warrior whispered excitedly, 'He did! I knew he would!'

'Did what?'

'The stick . . . the old horse tender threw it away when the bugle sounded. There!' The sharpened stick had fallen near the hay. 'If I could just get to it. We could use it as a weapon.'

'The bugle must mean Falcon Man or my father are out there.'

'Surely they would not attack the fort now with the wagon guns in place.' Little Warrior was silent for a long time. 'Bird Hunter, can you see the wall where the smoke rises from the dirt house?'

Bird Hunter moved to the window and looked past the smaller man. 'What is there to see? The wagon gun?'

'I saw Spotted Wolf crawling along the white guards' walk.'

'I don't see any one. Not even soldiers.'

'I know I saw him,' he exclaimed. But he could no longer see any movement. His chief would think he was empty-headed. Then a face popped in front of the window. The man jumped back, frightened. It was Squirrel.

'There is a chain on the door I cannot break without making noise. The guard ran when the horn sounded. How can I help you?'

'Give me your knife if you have another weapon. At the edge of the hay is a stick, too, that the white horse tender has carved.'

Squirrel passed the knife through the bars to Bird Hunter. When he found the sharpened stick, he passed it through the bars also. 'I have my war club, which is all I will need. Falcon Man, Peta Nocona, Little Mountain and your father are waiting. A Choctaw who was a trail finder for the soldiers is with us. He and Spotted Wolf are trying to destroy the wagon guns. They will try to plug the hole where the soldiers light the powder.'

CHAPTER TWENTY-SEVEN

'Oh, my God!' Major Daily had climbed to the lookout post on top of the building. 'Hundreds of them!' he yelled. 'On all sides!' He waved wildly to the colonel below. 'All around us, sir. Five or six hundred Indians.'

The exact count outside the walls waiting for a command from their chiefs were five hundred and fifty-four Comanche and Kiowa braves. Inside the walls were four armed Comanches and one Choctaw, who would be a man before the day ended.

Major Daily returned rapidly to the ground. 'What are your orders, sir?'

A bugle sounded the assembly call just outside the walls. Men from all parts of the wall sprang down the ladders to fall in on the drill field. His face flushed red, the colonel ran onto the drill field, waving his hands above his head.

'Go back to your posts! Go back! Go back!'

Major Daily summoned the bugler. 'Sound call to arms!'

The confused troops returned to their posts. But not before thirty of Falcon Man's best bowmen had rushed forward to a concealed position along the outside base of the wall.

'Lieutenant Collier! Man the west gun!' Major Daily ordered in a loud, calm voice. 'Bugler, if any other call sounds, repeat the call to arms. Sergeant! Find out where the other damn horn is!'

'Major Daily!'

'Yes, Lieutenant?'

'The gun has been spiked, sir. It is useless.'

'Check the north gun! On the double!'

A warrior named Small Man Leaning placed the spike in the touch hole, ready to drive it home when a pistol shot rang out, and Small Man Leaning fell beside the big gun. A smile crept over his face as he slipped into unconsciousness. Near him, Spotted Wolf crawled over to finish the job but a second shot rang out and he fell.

* * *

'I know I saw Spotted Wolf.' Little Warrior held the wooden weapon at his side ready for the door to open.

'There is the sound of the horn again,' Bird Hunter said.

Again the bugle sounded assembly. This time only a few soldiers were tempted to respond to the call when a contradictory order sounded from the bugle inside the fort.

'I feel useless!' complained Bird Hunter but he caught sight of Swede and McLin entering the fort. Both men rode quickly to the headquarters building and were lost from sight.

From his position on the hill, Falcon Man watched his bowmen as they crept along the wall toward the small gate which the Choctaw had opened for them.

Assuring himself that things were going as planned, Falcon Man called for six braves. 'Draw brush behind your horses and make much dust. The wind will carry it into the fort and make it ready for the torch.'

* * *

'Dust . . .' Bird Hunter said to Little Warrior. 'Why are they doing that?'

'When the dust settles, there will be no moisture left in anything. The fort will burn easily. The soldiers on the wall will be dying of thirst. Our chief is a very wise man.'

Squirrel was back at the window. 'The Choctaw and Spotted Wolf may be dead. What do you want me to do, Bird Hunter?'

'See if there is a horse in the stables. With chains or ropes of the white men, we could pull the bars from the wall.' Squirrel raced for the stables.

* * *

In the center of the drill field near the colonel, Lars dismounted. 'See what you have done! There are enough Indians out there to destroy you, this fort and the town. If there are any survivors, I hope you are one of them so you will have to answer for this.'

'It won't be before I hang two of them.'

'You haven't learned a thing! When you are wrong, you stick by it until the last grave will be dug.'

'Major Daily, get this damn civilian out of here. I want to know who opened the gate. Get a man up there to drill that touch hole open so we can use that west gun.' He had already dismissed Lars and Major Daily from his mind.

'Colonel, Mr. Swensen can talk to the Indians for us. He is the only one here who speaks Comanche.'

Dust settled on the colonel, making his red face more grotesque and his throat scratchy. 'Tell those Indians to get the hell out of here and leave army business to the army.'

'When you prepare to hang one of their chiefs, it *is* their business. I will not take that message to them. I will take their men out with me and relay your apology,' Lars said, feeling more in control.

'Savages ride in with a captive girl after they've murdered her whole family and you expect me to turn them loose and apologize?

Are you crazy, mister?' The colonel puffed up like a mating grouse. 'Sergeant, bring me the prisoners. I'll hang them here and now, by God.'

'That will really prove you're a fool. They have already proved they are better soldiers than you are. In your own fort, they spike a cannon while you strut and fume about hanging two of them. These men came to you to apologize and to explain that they had banned Killer of Women, the man guilty for the death of the girl's family. But faced with the truth, you still want to go on with your fool plans. So do it. I'll do everything in my power to keep you alive until after they have overrun this fort and killed everybody in it. Then I'll join in their festivities when they deal with you.

'Major, can't you do something? Relieve the colonel. He is no longer able to command.'

'If I live through this, I would have no career in the army, Mr. Swensen, and that is the only life I have.' The major looked at the colonel and sighed deeply. 'Even if you are right, I can't do what you suggest.'

Suddenly an explosion came from the west wall.

The major gasped in shock. 'The blacksmith . . . tried to drill the touch-hole . . . without drawing the powder!'

War club ready, Squirrel ducked into

hiding when he heard the sergeant approach the guardhouse. The burly non-com unlocked the door and stepped aside for Bird Hunter and Little Warrior to come out. The sergeant and two guards were ready with their weapons. They expected some fight from the Indians. When there was none, the soldiers relaxed for an instant. It was then that Bird Hunter swung into action. He plunged Squirrel's knife deep into a guard's chest. Little Warrior snatched the rifle. Squirrel brought his war club down upon the back of the sergeant's head and there was the sound of cracking bones.

An explosion rocked the ground under them.

The colonel turned to run and came face-to-face with Little Warrior. Before the colonel could defend himself, the young warrior wrapped his arm around the fat neck and held the sharp stick against it.

'At ease!' The major shouted, so that no one who had his rifle trained on Little Warrior would fire.

'Talk . . . please . . .' The colonel's throat was nearly paralyzed with fear.

'Will you talk to him, Mr. Swensen?' the major asked.

'Why should I talk to him? When the Indians wanted to talk, he didn't choose to do so. Now let him sweat.'

Bird Hunter walked onto the drill field

followed closely by Squirrel. He kept careful watch on the soldiers along the wall and in the compound. No one moved among them. Dust billowed over the walls and settled everywhere. The men in their blue uniforms took on a ghostly appearance.

Swensen embraced Bird Hunter. 'Are you all right?'

'There is nothing wrong with me that his scalp wouldn't make right.'

The color drained from the colonel's face when Swensen repeated what Bird Hunter had said.

'Can I kill him, Bird Hunter?' asked Little Warrior.

'If you do, you will have no shield.'

'He would not listen to us. When Falcon Man rides through the gate, can I kill him?' His arm tightened on the colonel's throat. 'Now he shows his true courage. He has emptied his bladder!'

'No need to kill him,' Bird Hunter said. While the soldiers were watching the compound, Slayer of Enemies' braves slipped through the small gate. There were many bows with strung arrows aimed at the blue coats.

'Lars, tell the fat soldier chief my worthy warrior will release him if he will not try any foolish tricks. Many braves of Slayer of Enemies are inside the fort and await my command to kill his men before they can fire their guns.'

The soldiers, facing more than thirty braves with their arrows ready, were near panic.

'We'll talk,' gasped the colonel.

Bird Hunter motioned for Little Warrior to release his captive. The colonel stepped back, rubbing his throat, taking his first few breaths with difficulty. Then with surprising speed for a man his size, the colonel drew his service revolver and fired. The bullet caught Little Warrior under his ribs. The wounded warrior lunged and sunk the sharpened stick into the colonel's neck.

When the commanding officer sprang into action so did the first sergeant nearby. He took quick aim at Bird Hunter's back. Lars Swensen stepped swiftly between his Comanche friend and the sergeant. Quickly the soldier lowered the revolver and the bullet slammed into the ground at Swensen's feet.

'Hold your fire! Hold your fire!' Major Daily yelled.

Slayer of Enemies' warriors relaxed the pressure on their bows as Bird Hunter lifted his arm to stop them. Kneeling beside Little Warrior, Bird Hunter checked his wound. 'Your action was a credit to you. It was as swift as the hawk flies, and I am proud of you. Be still so you will not bleed too much.'

Shaken, Major Daily spoke with a trembling voice. 'Mr. Swensen, tell your friends I am sorry for what has happened here. The colonel's action was not honorable. Our surgeon will treat the young warrior.'

The army surgeon made sure that the colonel was dead and there was nothing he could do for him. He straightened slowly. 'I'll see to the young man.'

'Major! Major Daily, sir!' shouted a lookout. 'There must be a thousand of them at the wall.' The major turned helplessly to Swensen. 'Can you do anything, sir?'

'Bird Hunter, will you reason with your people?' Lars asked.

'Open the big gate so my chiefs can speak for themselves. But the new soldier chief must give us his word there will be no reprisals.'

Lars translated for the major. The officer called out orders and the soldiers lowered their weapons.

'Sound assembly, bugler.'

An echo of the bugle call drifted from the outside walls.

'Open the gate!' bellowed the major.

Falcon Man entered, horse prancing, followed by Peta Nocona, Little Mountain, and Slayer of Enemies. They halted in front of the doctor who worked skillfully over the fallen brave. Seeing Slayer of Enemies, Swensen's face lit up.

'Father of my friend, it is good to see you again, although I am sorry we meet this way.

Little Warrior will surely be all right. The army doctor is very good and does not seem overly concerned about his recovery.'

The walls were now completely lined by armed braves who were undoubtedly disappointed that there was not to be a battle. For the first time Lars saw where the cannon had been. Two blue-coated bodies were sprawled grotesquely near the big splintered gun.

'Who will speak for the soldiers?' Falcon Man asked.

The major stepped forward, stood stiffly at attention beside the chief's horse.

'Major Daily is the commanding officer now and will speak for the soldiers.'

'Tell him we are very angry. My braves will be very disappointed if I do not allow them to kill every man, woman and child *here* and in the white village. It is not the wish of the older chiefs among my people or our friends, the Kiowas, that we make war.' He lifted his hand and pointed at Little Mountain. 'Our friends have had many problems with the whites crossing their lands. When the red man attempts to defend his home, the white soldiers come and kill him. We, the Comanche, will no longer stand by and allow this to happen. Nor will the Kiowa allow it to happen to the Comanche.'

He waited for Lars to catch up, in English.

'Many young men like Bird Hunter believe

any day is a good day for dying if they are defending their homes. Unless the young warriors of the white soldiers feel the same way, it will be a big mistake for you to make war with us. My heart would be heavy to watch the dying of your young men and ours, but I will ask it of the other chiefs if I must.' Falcon Man held his hand over his heart. 'Tell him these things, Swede, and tell him too that I will gladly be one of the first to die so I do not have to watch this thing. Yet there will be another stronger, younger, braver than I to take up the fight as long as his people or mine shall live.' He paused, his voice tired.

'We will ride from here today in peace. How long the peace lasts is up to you.'

Waiting for Lars to give him Falcon Man's final words, the major removed his hat humbly. 'Tell the chief as long as I have the power, there will be no attacks from this fort against his people or the Kiowa. We wish only to live in peace, and we honor his words.'

When Swensen had translated, the tribal chiefs conferred with Falcon Man in whispers. Then Peta Nocona spoke firmly to the Swede. 'Tell the white chief we will go when we have collected our dead and wounded. Also the body of the brave Choctaw who was one of his and became Comanche will go with us.'

Major Daily, nodding, agreed.

With a sweep of his arm, Slayer of Enemies commanded, 'Collect our dead and wounded and we will leave in peace.'

Silently the Comanche braves lifted Small Man Leaning and Spotted Wolf's bodies. Bird Hunter helped Little Warrior to his horse and the procession moved slowly toward the open gate. Soldiers lined up in formation, and Little Warrior held his head high. He would like to have taken the scalp of the white chief, but his brothers knew and would sing of him around the fires. At last he would be a man among men.

They would also sing of the Choctaw named Small Man Leaning who would rest forever among the honored dead of the Comanches.

And they would sing of the blond white man, Swensen, who had stepped in front of Bird Hunter to save him and was his strong medicine.

CHAPTER TWENTY-EIGHT

Bird Hunter rode beside his father and Falcon Man into the new village.

His wife Fawna ran to greet him. She touched him with longing while no one was watching, waiting for the village to honor her brave husband before they could be alone.

There were more lodges than when Bird Hunter had left. The women had rebuilt seemingly out of nothing.

At the circle of fire the chiefs turned their horses over to the aged Tender of Horses. Bird Hunter wondered if someday he might be the tender of horses when he was too old to protect his people from enemies.

'We have two dead and one wounded. In the fort they bury six,' Falcon Man boasted.

'Two of us were killed in the crippling of the wagon gun. The brave who was a Choctaw destroyed the killing spirit of the gun. We will sing of him and our women will cry for him. We will sing and cry for Spotted Wolf. We will also sing of Shivering Man's son, Little Warrior, because he is a brave man. He will sit at the fires of the braves, no longer a novice, not a man-boy but from this day on looked upon as a man among men. We will also sing of Bird Hunter for he has again proven himself worthy.' Falcon Man finished his speech and called to his wife. 'Is there food, woman? The sound of my stomach has been like a pack of dogs since first light.'

His wife ran to tend the cooking fire. With a pat on Bird Hunter's back, he said, 'We will talk again when we have seen two more suns. That is enough time for the manliest of men.'

Bird Hunter took Fawna's hand on the way to their lodge. 'It is my desire to hold the hand of the Kiowa girl named Fawna.'

'There is no Kiowa girl named Fawna. There is a Comanche woman called Fawna who is going to have a baby.'

He could hardly believe what he had heard. But the look in her eyes told him she was not teasing.

'You are sure?'

'Who would know better than I?'

Scooping her into his arms, he whirled her around. 'I am to be a father,' he announced in a loud voice to the people around them. 'Fawna is with child!'

'Put me down. You embarrass me. You will have to feed with the dogs.'

'Then why is there a smile behind your eyes and lips? I will teach him to pull a strong bow, to be the best hunter, to throw a lance, to . . .'

'What if it's a girl?'

There was a moment of silence while he pondered the thought. Then he leaned closer to his wife. 'She will be as pretty as her mother. She will drive all the young braves crazy. But one thing will be different. When the time comes, she will marry the man she desires, even if he has no horses!'

Fawna studied her husband. She was lucky to have such a man. It was her wish also that a daughter should marry the man she desired, not a man because he had many horses. Other women surely envied her because she was the wife of Bird Hunter. It was she who reached for his hand as they almost ran toward their lodge.

★ ★ ★

The time for crying had ended. Life settled in a soft peace that was gradually accepted but not fully trusted. It was the year of the white man, 1853. Texas days were warm and the nights cool in the Moon of the Browning Grass. Leaning against a tree, Bird Hunter counted his horses as they grazed beyond the creek. No man in his tribe had more horses than he. But he would give up every horse he had if it would relieve the pain Fawna was now bearing in childbirth. Fawna's mother had chased him away from the lodge.

'There is nothing you can do. Go! I will call you when you are a father.' So he waited and asked the Great Spirit to help.

Allowing his thoughts to drift like smoke on a warm wind, he did not at first see Dataha, tired but walking quickly toward him. There was a smile on her face.

'There will be much singing around the fires about Bird Hunter from this day on.'

'Why?' He gave her a mock frown. 'Speak up, woman, why have you come here? Just to disturb me?' he said with false gruffness.

'I have come to tell you . . .' She paused, drawing out the suspense.

'What? What?'

'You have *two* sons!' Her smile spread all over her face and her eyes closed with the fullness of it.

'Two sons? Did you say, two sons?'

'Yes. Two! They fill the lodge with their crying. It is enough to drive the hearing from you. I can hear the songs they will sing about the manly Bird Hunter who excels in everything, not just hunting and battle.' She laughed heartily.

'This is not one of your jokes? What you tell me is the truth?'

'The truth. Two of them and Fawna is well. It is good she has two places to feed them. You are lucky she did not have *three* babies.'

Kneeling beside his wife, he held her hand as her mother wiped her forehead with a cold cloth dipped in the creek. 'She is well?'

'Of course I am,' Fawna replied. 'What do you think of the Kiowa girl now? Did you get enough sons from her?'

'The Comanche woman Fawna is the most important person in this world to me. I would have given up all my horses if it would have taken the pain away.'

'All of your horses? What kind of warrior would you be if you had to walk to get to battle?'

'The white man's army has soldiers who walk. They are very good warriors. I could be as good as they are.'

'Of course you could if you arrived in time for the fight. But there is no need for you to give up your horses. Now that your sons are here, there is no pain.' She nodded toward the robes beyond the fire pit. 'Have you looked at your boys?'

Still on his knees, he pulled the robes open where his sons slept. They were beautiful but he could not tell them apart. 'They are too much alike. How will I know which is which?'

'When they are old enough to answer to their names, you will know. Until then, we must look for things that are different.'

He returned to sit beside her. 'Are you sure you are all right?'

'Very tired. And there will be a time that you cannot share my robes. Two moons, my mother has said. Perhaps you will want to take a second wife?'

'I have a wife. One wife is all I need. My father has but one wife. Peta Nocona has but one, and she is white.'

'True, but Many Wives has six wives now. Falcon Man has three. There are many men among our people who have more than one wife.'

'What have I ever done that would make you think I need or want more than one wife? We will speak no further of this.'

'Look around you. Have you no eyes?

There are more men and women in our tribe than there are children. What will happen to our people? There are girls who have been old enough for marriage for many seasons yet they have no husbands. Where will their babies come from?'

'You are enough.'

'Go to Dataha. She is a widow and it is permitted, as you well know. Kato asked you to. If she gets big, then you can marry her if you like. We would be like sisters. It is rumored that a Kiowa brave of the Pleasant Moon tribe has asked her to come with him.'

'There is nothing wrong with her taking a Kiowa. I now have two sons because I took one.'

'I don't want her to go away.'

There was a long silence between them.

Outside they could hear an impatient Slayer of Enemies.

'I want to see my two fine grandsons.'

Bird Hunter pushed back the flap of the tipi. 'You are welcome to come in.' Slayer of Enemies entered and Bird Hunter stepped outside into the sunlight, where Dataha tended meat at the fire pit.

'I wish to walk and talk with you,' he said uncomfortably. 'We will walk in the woods along the stream.'

'Yes,' she said simply and fell in beside him as he walked toward the path to the stream where the women filled their water bags.

They walked along the water's edge for a long time. Neither of them spoke. Water skipped and flowed over the rocks, making what his mother had often called the 'Water Songs.' Finally he broke the silence.

'Fawna has talked about you becoming my second wife.'

'Yes . . . if you want me.'

'The son of Kato walks now. He needs a father to teach him how to hunt and you need someone to provide for you.'

'There has always been room in my heart for you, Bird Hunter, even when we were children.'

Bird Hunter's eyes were troubled. 'Since all the chiefs gathered to attack the fort to free me and Little Warrior, there has been no trouble with the whites. Little Mountain allows them to cross his land and has no problems. It is not the way of the whites. Soon I will go see my friend Swensen and we will talk. It is difficult to rest. In my bones I feel that all is not right.'

'Those are the worries of the old, and you are not old.'

'Perhaps not in my body but in my mind sometimes I think I am older than my father and Falcon Man together, and it is not restful.'

CHAPTER TWENTY-NINE

'Is that you, Bird Hunter?' Fawna's voice was almost muffled in the robes drawn to her chin against the chilly wind.

Entering the tipi, he sat crosslegged on the edge of her robes. She was feeding one of the babies.

'They are never awake at the same time for their feeding. I feel I will never sleep again until they are eating at the fire with us.' She drew the robe back so he could see the child nuzzling her breast. 'He has the hunger of a man.'

She handed the sleeping baby to him. 'Put him with our other son and lie beside me for a while. I need to feel the warmth of you.'

Drawing her close to him, he warmed her and soon she was asleep. He listened to her soft breathing and would like to have slept too. But he could not. He went out into the night.

At dawn Bird Hunter spoke to Dataha. 'I'll talk to Falcon Man when the sun is up. You can move your lodge near Fawna's, and all will know that you are my second wife.'

'Fawna is like a sister to me already. We have laughed much together, and when you have been away in battle we have cried together.'

There was harmony between the two lodges and the two wives of Bird Hunter. He did not often have to come between them to prevent squabbles. Many Wives spent most of his time between two or more of his wives and often had to take a stick to separate them.

* * *

It had been four moons since the birth of his sons. Bird Hunter stirred the fire, adjusted the smoke hole at the top of the tipi. Fawna chewed a small piece of meat before feeding it to Red Feather. Bird Hunter could tell them apart now. He had tied a red feather on one son's wrist. Dataha held Black Feather, who wore around his tiny wrist the feather of a blackbird.

'It is good that you have marked them, Bird Hunter,' Dataha said. 'Even at a distance, we can tell them apart.' Dataha did not call him husband as Fawna did, respecting his first wife's right to do so. 'What will we do if I have two at the same time?'

Bird Hunter and Fawna turned quickly.

'Are you going to have a baby?' Fawna asked.

'Yes. When the leaves come back to the trees.'

Fawna leaned forward to pat Dataha's shoulder. 'The son of No Toe Foot is lucky.

He will have a brother . . . or a sister.'

'I hope it is a girl,' Dataha said. 'After all, there must be girls or there will be no Comanches.'

Bird Hunter smiled. 'That is true. If you want a girl, then you have my permission to have a girl. We will name her Yellow Finch for Swede, who is my medicine.'

* * *

Bird Hunter sat with his family in the warm sunshine before their lodges.

A small girl eased timidly toward Bird Hunter.

Fawna said, 'You are Love Shadow, daughter of Tasha, are you not?'

The shy child nodded.

'You seem to have something heavy on your mind.'

She coaxed the child near her.

Love Shadow stretched out her arms to Bird Hunter. Held tenderly in her hands was a frightened grey bird, with the long tail of the bird who sings like all birds.

'He is broken,' she said, in tears. 'Can you fix him so he will not die? Then I can keep him for my own.'

Bird Hunter took the bird from the child's gentle hands and held it with a like tenderness. He cupped Love Shadow's chin in his hand and wiped her tear-filled eyes.

'A bird is like a Comanche, little one. He must live and die free. You would destroy his heart after we healed his wounds if you kept him a prisoner.'

She nodded understandingly with her chin still resting in his hand.

'Good. We will tend the wound. When he is well, you can set him free so he will be able to fly with his own kind. Then Fawna will make a corn husk doll for you to keep for your own.'

Using several stiff trimmings from a willow branch, Bird Hunter mended the mockingbird's wing and gave him back to the child. 'You will need to feed it until we can remove the sticks when his bones have healed. Will you do that?'

Again Love Shadow nodded, smiling. Bird Hunter knew more about birds than anyone in the village. Now that he had fixed the wing, she would feed it until it could fly again.

As Love Shadow left, The Man Who Shivers in the Sun limped toward Bird Hunter.

'What is wrong, Man Shivering?'

'In the night I awakened with bad dreams about my son Little Warrior. He is long overdue from his horse raid on the Osage. I was going to look for him today, but cannot even get on my horse.'

'I will go find him for you. I need to get

away from women and babies. Soft living has made my belly too large. Soon it will take one whole buffalo to make a shirt for me.'

Man Shivering could hardly smile, he felt such foreboding.

'Have no fear. I will find him.' Bird Hunter rose to his feet and glanced down at his two women. There was sudden fear in their eyes. 'Stay with my family and watch my sons, Man Shivering. You cannot yet see her, but I have a daughter.'

* * *

Bird Hunter rode north toward the lands of the Osage. Squirrel and Stealer of Army Horses went with him. On the rump of the forward horse was the U.S. army brand with a bright red circle painted around it. It seemed to bring more challenge to the rider to know that he could be hung if the white soldiers caught him with this horse. The brand could easily be seen painted red.

Bird Hunter drew his horse to a halt. Squirrel reined up beside him and Stealer of Army Horses stopped also.

'What is wrong?'

'Something tells me our little friend is not in the land of the Osage. We will rest here while the spirit speaks to me.' He slipped from his horse, and left it ground-tied, to walk apart from the others. While they made camp, Bird Hunter brooded alone. Night fell. The wind grew colder. He drew his robe around him, still in silence.

For a moment he might have dozed. It was dark and he suddenly jumped up from his robes, calling to his companions.

'Little Warrior is not with the Osage. I saw him in the east sitting beside a fire. There was a binding on his chest and leg, as my father was bound when I left him with the white man's woman.'

'How can you be sure?'

'I saw him. Swede was with him. They will soon seek our village. We will go to the Swensen ranch.'

Through the night they rode as hard as their mounts could bear. Before the sun was up they were approaching the ranch. Smoke rose against a fading sky. From the ridge overlooking the ranch house and yard, the three Comanches could see only Osage. Enemy braves cast eerie shadows in the firelight from the burning barn. They were preparing to set the house afire also.

Three Comanches would have to outwit the small band of Osage. They would need to sound and fight as many.

Squirrel and Stealer of Army Horses watched their chief and followed his lead. When his heels dug into his horse's flanks, theirs did the same. They charged with the courage of many down the hill and into the yard. The valley echoed with the Comanche war cry.

The Osage were unprepared for such an onslaught. They were on foot and almost defenseless against the lance and war clubs wielded by the trio that came among them. Three of them died almost as soon as they were aware of the Comanches.

When the battle ended, Bird Hunter lay gravely wounded, the Osage axe buried in his chest.

CHAPTER THIRTY

Fearfully Stealer of Army Horses knelt beside his chief, who lay motionless in the yard beside his fallen horse.

The front door flew open and a hysterical voice cried, 'Don't touch him!' The white woman ran across the yard, her skirts held high so she could run faster. Lumbering behind her from the house was a big blond man. Slowly Stealer of Army Horses sank back on his moccasins as the woman knelt beside Bird Hunter.

'He's alive, Lars. Tell them to pick him up in the same position he's in now and carry him in the house.'

'Move back, Alfa. His horse isn't dead. He's going to come up from there in a minute like ten thousand tornadoes.'

'Kill him then. So he won't. He could kill Bird Hunter if he kicks coming up.'

Instantly the Swede wheeled and shot Bird Hunter's horse. Then he repeated his wife's orders to the Comanches, explaining how to move the chief's body into the house. Standing in the doorway was Little Warrior bandaged as Bird Hunter had seen him in his dream.

'We are in the way. Let's take a look at the damage while Alfa tends Bird Hunter.'

The Comanches seemed reluctant to leave their chief on the white man's bed, but they followed. The barn would be days burning.

'Why did you have two houses?' Stealer of Army Horses asked.

The Swede remembered years before when Bird Hunter had asked a similar question.

'This was the barn. The house for my horses.'

'Your horses have a house?' Their amazement was no less than their chief's had been. But the Comanche glanced repeatedly toward the house where their chief lay wounded. Already they had lost interest in the barn.

Holding his hand over the wound in his side, Little Warrior spoke from the front porch. 'It was not my intent to lead the Osage here, Lars. I am sorry I caused all of this. My chief would not be near death, and you would have your barn. You would not have the cut on your face from an Osage arrow.'

Swensen sighed, 'Don't blame yourself, Little Warrior.'

Stealer of Army Horses spoke to Little Warrior. 'We will sing for our chief so that he can return to his wives and sons. We will make our fire in the yard and you can tell us how this happened.'

Sitting beside their fire, the three Comanches sang softly:

'He is a warrior strong and brave;
  Our people need chiefs such as he.
We ask Great Spirit his life to save
  To keep our sons and daughters free.'

Alfa Swensen bent over the jagged wound. There was bleeding deep inside. At her feet lay the Osage axe she had carefully removed from Bird Hunter's chest. 'Shanda, dissolve some salt in hot water to clean the wound. Lars, heat a knife red hot and keep it that way. I need some heavy thread and my largest needle.' She glanced up and saw Bird Hunter watching her.

'He's awake. We need something to help him bear the pain.'

'Bird Hunter, Alfa is afraid she will hurt you.'

'Her hands . . . like the kiss of sunlight . . . on a cold day. No one tends . . . wound better than . . . beautiful white one. Worth wound . . . her attention.' He tried to smile.

Lars translated for Alfa, then added, 'I am a fool to relay such poetry to my own wife from another man.'

Every lamp in the house was lit and placed on the table at the bedside while Alfa sewed the wound.

'Most men would be bellowing with pain,' she said.

'Maybe he is numb.'

'No, I don't think so.'

Shanda waited quietly to help when she could. Tears flowed unheeded down her cheeks. 'Is he going to be all right?'

'Only time will tell. By morning, he will be burning with fever. That will be the worst time. It will be days before we know.'

Near dawn Bird Hunter's face was hot and dry, his lips cracked as fever raced through his body. Shanda and Alfa took turns keeping his brow and face washed in cold water. Under his breath he mumbled the same words over and over. 'Red Feather, Black Feather, Daughter of Dataha.'

'What is he saying, Lars?' Alfa asked, her brow wrinkled with concern.

'I can't make it out. I'll ask Little Warrior.'

Little Warrior stood with Lars at the foot of the bed. 'He is calling the names of his sons. Twin sons. Red Feather and Black Feather.' Little Warrior looked puzzled. 'But

I don't know what he means by "daughter of Dataha." Her child is a boy.'

The lamps in the house cast yellow light on the windows. In the yard, the chanting around the fire continued in hoarse whispers. A low fire lit the faces of three grieving men as the pale outline of a full moon emerged from the clouds.

Stealer of Army Horses raised his head to listen. From the top of a large cypress tree came the song of a mockingbird.

'It cannot be. The bird of many voices does not sing at night. He is calling the spirit of our chief to join him.' He leaped to his feet.

'What do you plan to do?' Squirrel asked.

'I will kill him so he cannot call the spirit of Bird Hunter to fly away with him.'

'Killing one bird of many voices will not help. There will be another and another until they take him away. We can only pray the Great Spirit hears us more clearly than he hears the birds.'

Stealer of Army Horses sank back to the ground. Beyond the place where the horse house burned came the song of a nightingale, and beyond that the call of an owl. They returned to their chant, trying to sing louder than the birds. But they could still hear the bird voices.

⋆ ⋆ ⋆

Squirrel groomed his horse. He waited to take word to the people of his village but wanted to be able to tell them Bird Hunter would live. So for three days he had waited.

Stealer of Army Horses came toward him, his head bowed. 'Ride to the village. Tell Slayer of Enemies to come quickly, his son is dying in the home of the white man Swede.'

'No! He cannot die! He is Bird Hunter. Who will lead us when the old chiefs are dead?'

'The white woman said he would die when the moon was high if the fire inside, the fever, is not broken. But already the sun is slipping and his skin still burns. Take three horses and for once do not spare them. I would go, but you are smaller and will be less burden for the horses.'

Squirrel mounted and held the rein of two extra horses in his free hand. As he dug his heels into the flanks of his horse and charged forward, Swensen burst from the ranch house, shouting and jumping wildly from the porch into the yard.

'He'll live! The fever is broken! Bird Hunter will live!'

Photoset, printed and bound in Great Britain by
REDWOOD PRESS LIMITED, Melksham, Wiltshire